CH
RIVI

JENNIFER MCGRATH KENT

Thank you for you
JUN 0 4 2010

NIMBUS
PUBLISHING

DEDICATION

This book is dedicated to Connor and Brennan, who are my
daily inspiration. And to Brian, my motivation.

And to Emily and Clare, And Eli and Grayson, of course.

This book is also dedicated to
The Riverview Fire and Rescue Department
and to
The police officers and EMS personnel of
The Greater Moncton Tri-Community

Copyright © 2007 Jennifer McGrath Kent

All rights reserved. No part of this book may be reproduced, stored in a retrieval system
or transmitted in any form or by any means without the prior written permission from the
publisher, or, in the case of photocopying or other reprographic copying, permission from
Access Copyright, 1 Yonge Street, Suite 1900, Toronto, Ontario M5E 1E5.

Nimbus Publishing Limited
PO Box 9166, Halifax, NS   B3K 5M8
(902) 455-4286

Printed and bound in Canada
Interior design: Kathy Kaulbach, Touchstone Design House
Front cover design: Cathy MacLean
Author photo: Lynne Post

Library and Archives Canada Cataloguing in Publication

Kent, Jennifer McGrath
Chocolate River rescue / Jennifer McGrath Kent.
ISBN 13: 978-1-55109-600-1
ISBN 10: 1-55109-600-5

1. Rescues—Juvenile fiction. 2. Petitcodiac River (N.B.)—Juvenile fiction. I. Title.
PS8621.E645C47 2007   jC813'.6   C2007-900984-0

Canada The Canada Council | Le Conseil des Arts
for the Arts | du Canada

NOVA SCOTIA
Tourism, Culture and Heritage

We acknowledge the financial support of the Government of Canada through the Book
Publishing Industry Development Program (BPIDP) and the Canada Council, and of the
Province of Nova Scotia through the Department of Tourism, Culture and Heritage for our
publishing activities.

TABLE OF CONTENTS

The Chocolate River

At the centre of the arena, two robots rolled toward each other. One robot raised a spinning saw blade. The other snapped a set of massive metal jaws. Then, with a sudden electric whine, both machines shot forward. The watching crowd roared. There was a screech of metal, a shower of sparks, and—

CLICK.

Both robots disappeared.

"Awwww, Mom!"

Mrs. Mahoney put down the remote. "That's enough TV for one day, boys. Time to go outside."

"But we're missing the best part!" protested nine-year-old Craig Mahoney from his pillow fort under the coffee table.

"Yeah, Mom," said Shawn. "It's the final round. If Saw-Blade knocks out Metal Mouth, he wins the championship!" Shawn was three years older than Craig, but shared his little brother's passion for watching *Battlebots* on Saturday afternoons. Shawn liked to see how the robots were built. Craig liked to see them come apart.

"And besides," argued Shawn, "*Battlebots* is educational—it's on the Learning Channel."

"Nice try," said his mother, "but I'd rather you get an outdoor education just now."

Shawn's best friend, Tony, poked his head out of the blanket tent he had constructed under the ping-pong table. "But Mrs. Mahoney, Saturdays were *invented* for watching TV!"

"Too much TV will rot your brain," said Mrs. Mahoney lightly, as she swept empty juice boxes and bread crusts onto a tray and headed back upstairs. "It's a gorgeous day outside. Go out and play."

"*Awwwww!*" said all three boys.

"There's nothing to do outside," complained Shawn.

"I'll give you something to do," said the boys' father, walking into the room. Mr. Mahoney was dressed in a parka and boots. He carried a snow shovel in one hand and his toolbox in the other. "The driveway needs to be shovelled. Then I'm going to build some extra shelves so we can clean up the garage. And somebody needs to put out the trash and sort the recyclables. Who wants to help?"

"Um, come to think of it we *are* kind of busy," said Shawn, backing away. "We have, uh, *stuff* we need to do today…don't we, Tony?"

"Oh. Uh, right," said Tony, catching his friend's warning look. "The stuff—I almost forgot. Important stuff that, uh, needs doing. Right now. So long, Mr.

Mahoney!" He dashed upstairs with Shawn hot on his heels.

"Wait up, guys!" called Craig, pounding up the stairs after them. "I'll help you with the stuff too!"

The front door slammed three times.

"Works every time," smiled Mr. Mahoney.

Upstairs, Mrs. Mahoney leaned out her kitchen door and called after the boys.

"Shawn! Keep an eye on your brother…don't you and Tony go leaving him behind anywhere!"

"Okay, Mom!" yelled Shawn, giving her a wave over his shoulder. As if Craig would let himself get left behind, thought Shawn. That kid could stick to a person like Krazy-Glue.

Once they were out of sight of the house (and safely out of range from Mr. Mahoney and his list of chores), the boys slowed to a walk, scuffing their boots in the snow as they plodded along the sidewalk: one tall, quiet boy followed by two shorter, energetic boys who scuffled and wrestled with each other as they made their way down the street.

Tall and slender, with light brown hair, Shawn had grey eyes that always seemed to be looking at something far away. *Poet's eyes*, his mom called them, but that dreamy look usually meant that Shawn was just thinking up something to build. His room was full of his inventions. Like the catapult he'd built for flinging dirty socks and underwear across the room into his laundry hamper. Well, *sometimes* they landed in the laundry hamper. He had to work on his aim. Someday, Shawn thought, he'd design roller coasters for amusement parks.

And Craig could test them out.

A grin flickered across Shawn's face. His little brother loved anything that went fast. Craig would try just about anything once, thought Shawn, thinking of the time Craig had tried to go down the neighbourhood's steepest street—while standing on the crossbar of his bike. He still had the scars on his knees and elbows from that little adventure.

"So Shawn, what do you want to do today?" asked Tony, interrupting Shawn's thoughts.

"I dunno." Shawn reached up and tugged at an overhanging tree-branch, dumping a cascade of snow onto Craig's head.

"Hey!" protested Craig. "Whatddya do that for?" He scooped up a snowball and lobbed it at his brother. Shawn ducked and the snowball grazed Tony's ear.

Tony casually pushed Craig into a snowbank. "Come on, Shawn. You always have good ideas."

"I don't know," Shawn shrugged. The winter sky sagged above them, grey and heavy as a wet blanket. "What do *you* want to do?"

"*Mrrumph! Grrowfff!*" said Craig from inside the snowbank.

"I asked you first," said Tony, bouncing impatiently on his toes. Slightly shorter than his friend, with a spiky brush-cut that made him look a little like a hedgehog, Tony fairly vibrated with energy. Even if they were just hanging out, watching TV, Tony had to be moving: playing ping-pong or air hockey—or picking a pillowfight with Craig. At his own house, Tony had one of those mini-trampolines set up in front of his television so he could bounce while watching TV. There were scuff marks on the ceiling from the times he had bounced too high.

"Come on, we gotta do *something*. I'm about to die from boredom! Watch." Tony clutched his throat, making gagging noises and collapsed onto the sidewalk. He opened one eye and looked up at Shawn. "See? You're killing me here."

Shawn snorted with laughter.

"Let's go to the playground!" said Craig, finally flailing his way out of the snowbank. He stood up and shook the snow off his hat like a dog.

"Naw," said Shawn. He mashed a clump of slush with his boot. "The playground's no good in the winter."

"We could build a snow fort," suggested Tony.

"The snow isn't sticky enough," said Shawn, "and there isn't enough of it anyway."

"Not enough snow to go sliding, either," sighed Craig.

"We could play X-Box at your house, Tony," said Shawn.

"Uh-uh," said Tony, shaking his head. "My mom's book club is coming over today. It's like having a whole herd of librarians in your living room."

"Man!" said Shawn, "This day is so totally boring!"

"How about we go to the bridge?" said Craig.

The Gunningsville Bridge was new. It connected the town of Riverview, where the boys lived, to the City of Moncton, which was just across the river. Over the past year, the boys had watched, fascinated, as workers had dismantled the old, rickety bridge and replaced it — piece by massive piece — with a new concrete structure. The best part was that the new bridge had lookout points, where people could stop and just watch the river.

And the Petitcodiac was a river worth watching.

For one thing, it had the highest tides in the world. When the tide was out, the Petitcodiac was nothing more than a trickle at the bottom of the deep, muddy riverbed. But when the tide came in, it rushed in all at once, rolling up from the Bay of Fundy in a single wave called a tidal bore. And just like that, the Petitcodiac would change from a trickle to a deep channel of fast-moving, brown water.

Goodbye, stream. Hello, river.

It was that quick.

Later, the tide would go out almost as quickly as it had come in. Shawn always thought it was like someone had pulled the plug in a giant bathtub. The water would suddenly change direction and go slooshing back down the river, draining away into the sea:

Slurp.

Gurgle.

Gone.

Craig, Shawn and Tony ran down the street, skidding to a stop at crosswalk lights. Across the road was the bridge, spanning the river like a drawbridge over a moat.

"Hey, let me push the button!" said Craig, elbowing his way past the two older boys at the crosswalk and jamming his thumb against the red signal button.

"What's your rush? You going to a fire?" said Tony.

"Not yet," said Craig, grinning, "but I will be someday. I'm going to be a firefighter when I grow up."

"Hey, look, you guys," said Tony, "I'm breathing fire!" He blew and his breath came out as a puff of white smoke.

"Brrr, it's cold!" said Shawn, stamping his feet.

"Come on!" said Craig, "The light's changed."

The boys ran across the street, up the sidewalk and onto the bridge's walkway. They peered through the railing.

"There it is," said Tony. "The Chocolate River."

In summer, the Petitcodiac was the colour of hot chocolate. In winter, it looked like a chocolate milkshake, thick and slushy.

"Look, an iceberg!" said Craig, pointing at the water.

"There's another one!" said Shawn.

"That isn't an iceberg," said Tony. "It's too small to be an iceberg. Icebergs are huge and have penguins on them."

"Well, ice *chunks*, then," said Shawn, "and that one has a seagull on it. Look!"

"Ahoy, there!" shouted Tony, waving at the seagull as it sailed down the river. "Have a good trip!"

"Do you think that seagull will ride that piece of ice all the way to sea?" wondered Craig.

"It could," said Shawn, "if it wanted to. But if I were a seagull I'd get bored and fly away before I went that far."

"Yeah, bet he gets off at Deluxe Restaurant for some fish and chips," snickered Craig.

"Hey, check it out!" said Tony suddenly, "What's that over there?"

Below them, on the riverbank, something silvery was glinting in the snow.

On Thin Ice

"Is it money?" asked Shawn.

"I don't think so," said Tony, shielding his eyes with his hands and squinting at the shiny thing on the snow far below.

"It's probably just an old candy wrapper," said Craig.

"Let's find out!" said Tony, and he took off, sprinting back down the walkway.

"Hey, wait up!" called Shawn and Craig, running after him.

The three boys ran down onto the Riverfront Path, dodging a jogger and startling a lady walking a fat cocker spaniel. They stopped and peered down at the riverbank below the bridge.

"Where is it?" asked Shawn.

"There it is!" said Tony, pointing. He sat down and slid a little ways down the bank. "I can see it now. It's down there on the ice. It's a Manga Warriors card!"

"Really? Which one is it?" said Craig, sliding down next to him and craning his neck to see better. Craig loved trading card games. "Hey! That's Green-Eyes-Gold-Dragon…I need that one! Dibs!"

"Hey, no way! I saw it first!" protested Tony.

"Yeah, but you didn't know what it was. I recognized it first, so it should be mine," said Craig, stubbornly.

"No way. Finders, keepers!" said Tony.

"Uh-uh...*getters*, keepers," said Shawn, slipping past both of them and reaching for the foil card sticking out of the snow.

"No way! I saw it first! It's mine!" yelled Tony. With a whoop, he tackled Shawn from behind and both boys sprawled in a heap on the ice at the edge of the river.

"Hey!" spluttered Shawn. "Now I've got snow down my neck!"

"And I've got the card!" said a voice above them.

Tony and Shawn looked up from where they lay tangled on the ice. There stood Craig, holding up the card triumphantly.

"Too bad, guys," he grinned, waggling the card at them. "You snooze, you lose."

"Give it here!" said Tony, scrambling to his feet.

"Get him!" said Shawn, jumping up.

Laughing, Craig ducked underneath their outstretched arms and skipped out on the ice beyond their reach. "Come and get it!" he dared, sticking out his tongue at them.

Tony and Shawn looked at each other.

"He asked for it..." said Shawn, shrugging.

"Oh, yeah," said Tony. "And you know what that means..."

"*NOOGIE!!*" yelled both boys together, launching themselves at Craig. All three boys went down on the ice with a crash, shrieking and laughing. Shawn snatched Craig's hat and Tony rumpled the younger boy's hair with his knuckles until it was standing straight up.

"I give up! I give up!" gasped Craig, between giggles. "Lay off, you guys!"

Just then a shout made all three boys look up. A man, standing on the bridge above them, was waving frantically at them and shouting. Shawn stood up and waved back. "Hey—it's okay, mister!" he called. "We're not hurting him or anything…he's my brother. He doesn't mind!" He turned and punched Craig in the shoulder. "Craig, wave at him so he knows you're all right."

Grinning, Craig stood up and waved vigorously at the man on the bridge. The man pointed at them and shouted something else.

"What's he saying?" asked Tony.

"I dunno," said Shawn, perplexed. "Maybe he dropped something."

"Hey, maybe the card belongs to him," said Craig.

"Come on," said Tony, "What would a grown-up want Green-Eyes-Gold-Dragon for?"

Shawn shrugged. "Maybe it belongs to his kid?"

"He's coming down!" Craig pointed. The man had left the bridge railing and was running down the walkway toward the Riverfront Path.

"Is he coming after us?" said Tony nervously. The man ran off the bridge and began waving both arms at the passing traffic.

"Uh…what's he doing?" said Shawn, watching the man curiously.

"Beats me," said Tony.

A car slowed down and stopped.

It was a police car.

The car door opened and the boys watched as an officer got out and spoke with the man from the bridge. The man continued to point frantically in the direction of the boys. The police officer turned and looked toward the river. Then he started to run toward the boys. Fast.

"Oh man," breathed Shawn.

"We're in trouble now," said Tony.

"What for?" asked Craig, who had gone very white underneath his freckles. "What did we do?"

"They must really want this card," said Tony. "Shawn, do you think we're going to get arrested?"

CRACK!

The ground lurched beneath the three boys.

"What the—?" Craig dropped to his knees as the ground shifted again.

"The ice!" said Shawn, "It's breaking!" Shawn jumped off the ice back onto the snowy bank.

"Get up!" shouted Tony to Craig.

Craig scrambled to his feet.

KRRRRRICK!

A crack opened up right between Craig's legs. Brown water bubbled up between his boots.

"Shawn!" he screamed. There was a note of terror in Craig's voice that Shawn had never heard before.

"Get off of there, Craig!" shouted Shawn.

"I can't! I'm slipping!" wailed Craig.

Shawn leaped back onto the ice. He took a breath and jumped over the widening crack, grabbing his little brother by the coat as he flew through the air. Both boys fell heavily to the ice on the other side, landing next to Tony.

CRUNCH!

The ice bucked and a second crack appeared, licking through the ice like an electric current. The boys stared in horror as the crack widened to reveal an eddy of churning, foaming brown water.

"Jump for it!" yelled Tony. He took a step. The ice beneath their feet shuddered and tilted slightly.

"Stop! Don't move!" cried Shawn. "You'll tip us into the water!"

"But we're breaking away from the shore!" said Tony. "We've got to get off this thing!"

He was right. The crack was widening quickly. One end of the icy chunk started to swing in a slow arc toward the centre of the river.

"Shawn—!" moaned Craig. Shawn looked toward the bank. He saw the police officer racing toward them. The officer was stretching out his arms to them. He was yelling something. Now Shawn understood.

The police officer wasn't chasing them; he was trying to save them.

"Help!" he yelled at the police officer. "Help us!"

The officer was skidding and sliding down the bank now. He almost reached them…

SNNNICK–SPLASH!

The last piece of ice connecting them to the riverbank crumpled and collapsed into the water. The tabletop-sized ice floe dipped, bobbed…and spun slowly away from the bank. Throwing himself forward on his belly, the police officer made a grab for the edge of the ice floe—and missed.

As they drifted away into the channel of brown water, Shawn found himself staring into the horrified eyes of the RCMP officer…and realized with a shock that the officer looked as scared as he was.

CHAPTER

3

Not An Ordinary Day

Just outside of town, twelve-year-old Petra Harper was
banging at the front door of her uncle's log house. She
was dressed warmly in ski pants and boots. Her long
chestnut hair curled out from beneath her hat in two
loose pigtails. An old, battered pair of cross-country
skis was tucked awkwardly under one arm.

"Uncle Daryl?"

Petra leaned on the doorbell with her thumb and
squinted through the glass in the front door. Nothing.

He must be out in the garage, thought Petra. *I hope
he didn't forget what today is.* She shook her head.
Her uncle could get pretty absent-minded when he
was working on one of his projects. She stuck the skis
in a snowbank and headed around back.

Behind the house was a big double-door garage. It
had been a barn at one time, but her uncle had turned
it into his workshop. Daryl Harper was a firefighter,
but whenever he wasn't at work, he was tinkering
with tools and bits of machinery. His workshop was
his favourite place to be. Today was his day off, so it
made sense that Petra would find him there. Except
that today wasn't an ordinary day.

"He forgot. I just know it," muttered Petra to herself as she stomped toward the garage. She threw open the door. There stood her uncle with his back to her, bent over his table saw.

"Uncle Daryl!"

Her uncle jumped, dropping a piece of wood with a clatter.

"Petra, don't sneak up on me like that—I'm too young to have a heart attack!"

Petra put her hands on her hips. Her green eyes flashed. "You forgot, didn't you?" she said accusingly.

Daryl blinked at her through his safety goggles. "Forgot what?"

"My birthday!"

Daryl pushed the goggles up on top of his head and raised his eyebrows.

"Oh. Was that today?"

"Uncle Daryl! You promised to take me skiing on my birthday—remember?"

Daryl scratched his head, pretending to think. "Wait a minute…I think I do seem to recall something about…Ah, yes—that would explain what these are doing here." Reaching under his workbench, Daryl pulled out a pair of brand-new cross-country skis, wrapped in a red bow.

Petra's jaw fell open.

Then she launched herself at her uncle. "You didn't forget!"

Daryl staggered under his niece's loving assault as he gently tried to loosen her stranglehold around his neck. "Erk...Petra...must...breathe...now."

Giggling, Petra let him go and examined the new skis in delight. "They're perfect! Thanks, Uncle Daryl! These will go down the hills so fast!"

Daryl grinned. "Yep. And they're all waxed and ready to go. I'd never forget my favourite niece's birthday."

"I'm your only niece."

Daryl waved this minor detail aside. "Why don't you go put them in the truck?"

Petra dashed out to the driveway with the new skis...and stopped short.

"Uh, Uncle Daryl...did you know there's a boat on your truck?"

Hitched to Daryl's black-and-red pickup was a trailer. On the trailer was a boat, an inflatable Zodiac raft with a small outboard motor.

"Oh, yeah. Almost forgot about that," said her uncle following her outside.

"Is it a rescue boat?" asked Petra, curiously, running her hand along the black rubber sides.

"It was," said Daryl, bending down to check the trailer hitch. "It's retired now. The fire department just bought a new rescue raft. A bigger one. The Chief wants to keep this one around as a backup, but the motor's been acting up a bit, so I said I would take it home and give it a tune-up. I'll just unhitch it in a minute and put it in the garage."

"Maybe we could take it out on the lake later."

Daryl laughed. "Bit cold to be out on the water today, I think. How about we stick to skiing?"

"Okay. Let's go, then." Petra yanked open the door of the truck.

A huge black beast leaped out at her.

"*Ooff!*"

Two bear-sized paws hit her squarely in the chest and Petra sat down hard in the snow. Black jaws gleaming with long white teeth drooled just inches from her nose.

"Hobart!"

Giggling, Petra shoved at the great, shaggy head panting in her face. "Eewww! You've got dog breath, mister!"

Hobart, Uncle Daryl's big Newfoundland dog, flopped over onto his back and whined, waving a massive paw in the air apologetically.

Petra laughed. "Hobie, you big goof!" she said, reaching over to rub his belly. "Are you coming skiing with us?"

Hobart wriggled with joy and leaped to his feet with a thunderous *woof!*

"I take it that means yes," said Petra, standing up and brushing herself off.

"Hobart loves to go skiing," said Uncle Daryl. "I can't very well leave him behind—he'd be heartbroken."

"The more, the merrier," laughed Petra as the big dog pranced in clumsy circles around them. "He can tow me up the hills when I get tired." She patted the truck seat and Hobart hopped back in. Petra climbed in beside him and closed the door. "We're ready, Uncle Daryl."

"You're forgetting something very important," her uncle said seriously.

Petra wrinkled her brow in thought. "I've got my skis, poles, a water bottle and extra ski wax." She patted the fanny pack strapped around her waist. "Oh yeah—and the little first aid kit you got me for Christmas. What else is there?"

"Food," said her uncle, heading for the house.

"Got it covered," Petra called, waving a little snack baggy at him. "Trail mix. Mom made it this morning."

Daryl snorted and shook his head. "I just got off an eight-hour shift. I'm going to need more than a bag of birdseed to keep me going." He walked up the steps. "You and Hobart listen to the radio in the truck for a minute. I'll be right out." He disappeared into the house.

Petra reached across Hobart, who was happily drooling all over the dashboard, and clicked on the radio. Music came blaring out: "*Life is a hiii-iighway. I'm gonna riii-iide it all night looooong.*"

"*Oooo-oooo-oooo,*" Hobart howled.

"Wow, Hobie, you should be on *Canadian Idol*," said Petra, laughing. The song ended. There was a commercial for Crazy Al's Carpet Warehouse. Then the news came on: "*The government announced funding for a new literacy program today...*"

Petra turned off the radio. Beside her, Hobart panted quietly, fogging up the windows. It was quiet in the truck. Too quiet. Petra reached over and clicked on the scanner. The scanner was like a radio except that it picked up all the emergency calls and radio chatter from police cars, fire trucks, ambulances, and the 911 dispatcher.

Daryl liked having the scanner in his truck. That way he always knew if an emergency was in progress, even when he was off-duty. If something big happened, Daryl would go in to lend a hand, even on his days off. "I'm a firefighter 24/7," he liked to tell Petra. "I go whenever I'm needed. Kinda like Spiderman."

Petra fiddled with the dial on the scanner. Static crackled and hissed. Then a young man's voice came on. He sounded urgent and out of breath:

"*...stranded on an ice floe! I repeat: three boys stranded on an ice floe...Petitcodiac River...moving quickly! Request assistance immediately! Over!*"

The dispatcher's voice came over the scanner, answering him.

"*Repeat your location, please, Constable Belliveau.*"

"*I'm at the Gunningsville Bridge. Request assistance immediately! Tide's on its way out...*

They're moving fast! We're going to lose them…"
Static crackled over the radio. Then the young
officer's voice broke through again, sounding frantic.
"…almost out of sight…have to try to cut them off…"
Static hissed and buzzed, drowning out the officer's
words.

Petra was out of the truck, sprinting for the house.
"Uncle Daryl!"

Her uncle was just coming out the door. He was
carrying a big paper bag. He waved when he saw her:
"Hold your horses! I'm coming. I made us lunch—
two cheese and meatball subs, fully loaded. My
own secret recipe. Now that's what I call food!" He
stopped abruptly when he saw Petra's face. "What's
wrong?"

Petra skidded to a stop in front of him, panting puffs
of smoke into the frosty air.

"Just heard…on the scanner…something's
happened!" she gasped. Her uncle didn't wait to hear
more; he was already running for the truck.

A Thread of Hope

"Oh, this is bad," moaned Tony, shaking his head.
"Bad, bad, bad…"

Shawn and the police officer both stood as if frozen,
staring at each other across the ever-widening gulf of
chocolate-coloured water. The police officer turned his
head and began speaking urgently into a small radio
strapped on his shoulder. Then he scrambled back up
the bank, running toward the road.

"He's leaving us!" Shawn's voice came out
somewhere between a croak and a squeak. "The
officer's leaving!"

"Where's he going?" said Craig. "Why isn't he
helping us?"

The boys watched the police officer running to his
parked car. By now, other cars had stopped along
the road. Several people had gotten out and were
standing along the road, watching and pointing. The
ice floe carrying the boys swept past them all. Soon
the people standing by their cars were just tiny stick
figures in the distance.

"Help us!" Tony yelled at them. He turned to
Shawn. "Why doesn't somebody do something?"

"What are they going to do, dive in?" asked Shawn sharply. "The water's freezing. You'd die of hypothermia in about ten seconds."

Craig and Tony both looked at Shawn. For a long time, the only sound was the gurgling of the river and the snap-crackling of ice along its banks.

"But...who's going to help us?" whispered Tony. His face had gone very white.

Craig was staring at his big brother with an expression that was somewhere between shock and horror.

"We're going to drown, aren't we, Shawn?" he said in a low voice.

Shawn swallowed hard. "Not if we stay on this ice floe," he told his little brother. "We just have to hold very still and—and not fall off."

"But h-h-how are we going to g-g-get off?" asked Tony. His teeth were suddenly chattering so hard he could hardly talk.

"I don't know," said Shawn. "Maybe we'll run aground."

"We're about to run into something," said Craig, pointing. "But it isn't the ground! Look!" A huge chunk of ice was floating directly into their path.

"Hold on!" shouted Shawn.

"To what?" yelled Tony.

"Each other!" said Shawn.

Huddled in a tight circle, boots braced on the slippery ice, the three boys grabbed each other's arms by the elbows.

"Oh, man," said Tony. "Now I know how the *Titanic* felt!"

"Here it comes," warned Shawn. "Get ready: three…two…one…"

CRRR-UNCH!

The front corner of the ice floe dipped sharply, sending a wave of freezing brown water sloshing over the boys' boots. Craig yelled as his feet slipped out from under him. He landed hard on his knees. The ice floe pitched and rolled, sending more water sloshing around their feet.

"WHOAAAA!" yelled all three boys.

"Hang on! Hang on!" yelled Shawn. He and Tony hauled Craig back to his feet. The ice floe righted itself and resumed its journey downriver, spinning in lazy circles. For a long while the boys said nothing. They just stood, panting and shivering, clinging to each other in silent terror.

"Where are we?" asked Tony after a few minutes. "How far have we gone?"

Craig raised his head and looked. "We're closer to the Moncton side of the river," he said. "Look, there's the skate park!"

"What I would give to be on a skateboard right now instead of this stupid hunk of ice!" moaned Tony.

"Is anybody there?" asked Shawn, hopefully. "Maybe someone will see us."

"Not exactly skateboarding season, is it?" replied Craig. "Nope, nobody there."

The ice floe sailed on. The boys watched in silence as they travelled past the city parking lot, past the library, past the fancy restaurant with the patio lanterns, past the big iron statue of a ship's anchor in Bore Park. But it was a cold day. There was nobody at the park. There was nobody on the Riverfront Path. Nobody to notice three boys on a tiny chunk of ice slipping quietly and swiftly between the slick, frozen banks of the Petitcodiac.

"The hotel's coming up!" said Shawn. "Maybe somebody there will see us."

"Wait a minute!" Craig cocked his head. "Do you hear that?"

"I hear it!" said Tony.

"It's a siren!" said Shawn.

"It's the police officer!" yelped Craig, "He's coming to save us!"

Just above the riverbank, the boys could see the flashing lights of a police car. Then, as they watched, the car zoomed right past them at high speed.

"Hey!" shouted Tony, "Where do you think you're going? We're over here!"

"Come back!" called Craig after the disappearing car. "What's he doing, Shawn? Didn't he see us?"

"He saw us," said Shawn. "He also saw *that*—look!"

Tony and Craig craned their heads around to look where Shawn was pointing. Up ahead, a finger of ice jutted out from the muddy bank into the river. The police car braked hard and skidded to a halt. The police officer jumped out, scrambled down the bank and began running out along the finger of ice.

"He's trying to head us off!" said Shawn.

"We're not going to be close enough!" said Tony, "We're too far out!"

Up ahead, the police officer waited, standing at the very tip of his icy platform.

Tony squinted, shielding his eyes with his hands. "He's holding something."

"A rope!" said Craig excitedly. "It's a rope!"

Somewhere in the distance, more sirens were wailing, coming closer.

"We're saved!" whooped Tony.

Shawn looked around. Their ice floe was drifting out toward the middle of the river. Ahead, the police officer crouched, like a diver on the edge of a diving board—waiting. Shawn shook his head. "We're not close enough."

"Sure we are," said Tony, "he's got a rope. Ropes are long. We'll catch it and he'll tow us in. It'll work." Tony swallowed hard and peered anxiously ahead. "It's got to work."

"What happens if he misses?" asked Craig quietly.

"He won't miss!" said Tony loudly.

Shawn didn't say anything. Looking ahead, he saw that past the finger of ice where the officer stood, the Petitcodiac River widened and then curved sharply away from the city, cutting a brown line toward the empty, wind-swept marshes.

Shawn's thoughts drifted back to his classroom at school. Just last week, his class had begun working on their history projects. Lisa Boudreau, who sat in front of Shawn, was doing her report on the Petitcodiac River. Ms. Geldart, their teacher, had pinned a large map onto the bulletin board. It showed Riverview, Moncton, and Dieppe. A blue, twisty line snaked between Moncton and Riverview and turned a sharp corner at Dieppe.

"Who can tell me how the Petitcodiac got its name?" asked Ms. Geldart, tapping the twisty blue line on the map. The class exchanged looks. Some kids shrugged their shoulders. Nobody answered.

"Okay," said Ms. Geldart, smiling, "here's a hint: what language do you think the word 'Petitcodiac' comes from, and why?"

There was silence for a moment. Then Sarah Marsh, who sat near the front of the room, raised her hand slowly. "French? Because it has the word *petit* at the beginning, and *petit* is French for 'little,'" she said.

"Very good, Sarah," said Ms. Geldart. "And what does the shape of the river remind you of?"

"Um, a crooked branch?" said Pete Simmons.

"It kind of looks like an arm," said Lisa.

Ms. Geldart tapped the spot where the river bent sharply downward, "What part of an arm?" she asked.

"The elbow!" said Shawn.

"And what is the French word for elbow, class?"

The class was quiet for a minute, thinking.

"*Le coude!*" exclaimed Sarah suddenly. She was the best at French.

"*Petit coude*…little elbow!" chimed in Lisa. The class laughed. It was a funny name for a river.

"Right you are," said Ms. Geldart. "French Acadian settlers who lived along the river banks many years ago noticed the river bent like an elbow and the river was known by them as the Petitcodiac. But another group of people were also living along the river, a group of people who were there even before the Acadian settlers."

"The First Nations people!" said Pete.

"Right," said Ms. Geldart. "The Mi'kmaq people also named the river for its funny shape. They called it *Pet-Kout-Koy-Ek*, which is thought to mean 'River that bends like a bow.'"

"You mean as in bow and arrows?" said Shawn. "Cool!"

"Exactly," said Ms. Geldart. "And when the Mi'kmaq people told the Acadian settlers the name of their river…"

"The Acadians might have thought they were saying, "*Petit Coude-iac*," giggled Sarah. "Little elbow."

"It makes sense," said Pete. "Both names work: the river does bend like a bow and it does look like an elbow too!"

A wavelet of freezing brown water sloshed over Shawn's boot. And suddenly he remembered he wasn't sitting at his desk in a warm classroom anymore. He was on an ice floe in the middle of a very deep, very fast, very cold river.

"We're going around the bend," said Shawn, quietly.

"Tell me about it," said Tony. "I'm going to go around the bend if that officer doesn't throw that rope soon!"

"No," said Shawn, "I mean we've reached the elbow."

"What?" said Craig, through chattering teeth. "W-w-what are you talking about, Shawn?"

Shawn tried to explain. "If we don't catch the rope, we'll float around the bend in the river. After that, the river heads out across the marsh, away from the city. Away from the road. Get it? They won't be able to follow us anymore. We'll be out of reach."

Tony and Craig looked at Shawn.

They looked at the river.

They saw the bend.

"Paddle!" said Tony.

"With what?" yelled Craig.

"With our hands!" yelled Tony. He dropped to his knees and was about to plunge his mittens into the brown water when Shawn grabbed him by the shoulders.

"Don't, Tony! Your fingers will freeze. You'll get frostbite!"

"Yeah!" said Craig, "I saw a TV show about that, once. A mountain climber got frostbite and his fingers turned black and fell off!"

Tony snatched his hands away from the water. "You're making that up."

"Uh-uh," said Craig, shaking his head. "It was really gross."

Shawn nodded. "I saw it too. Discovery Channel."

Tony looked worried. "My feet are wet," he said.

"So are mine," said Craig.

"Mine, too," said Shawn.

The boys looked toward the police officer.

"Help!" they all shouted.

The officer waved and yelled something they couldn't quite hear.

They were almost level with him. The ice floe was moving fast, sweeping them past the icy banks. Closer and closer they sailed toward the narrow jetty of ice where the police officer stood, waiting for them.

"Now!" screamed Tony.

The officer raised his arm. He swung the rope around and around his head like a cowboy. He let go. The rope snaked through the air toward them. All three boys stretched out their hands.

The rope fell short. It landed in the water with a sad little smack.

"No!" shouted Tony, "No, no, no!"

The ice floe sailed on. Past the rope. Past the police officer. Around the bend.

The Chase is On

Trees and farmhouses flashed past Petra's window as
Uncle Daryl's pickup truck sped down the country
road toward Riverview. The trailer carrying the
Zodiac raft rattled and bounced along behind them.
Uncle Daryl hadn't taken the time to unhitch it when
he heard the news on the scanner.

With one hand, Daryl reached for the com radio
under the truck's dashboard.

"Reg, you there? Come in, Reg."

Reg was a firefighter on Daryl's crew. His job was
driving Rescue 10, a heavy, box-shaped fire truck
that responded to all rescue and accident calls. Its
compartments were filled with rescue equipment
for every possible emergency situation: First Aid
supplies, rappelling gear, chainsaws, axes, and even a
special saw that could cut through metal and concrete.
There were also air bags, oxygen tanks, ice suits, and
more.

The radio whistled and hissed. Then Reg's voice
came through the static, sounding tinny and crackly.
Over the radio, Petra could hear Rescue 10's siren
wailing in the background.

"This is Rescue 10. I hear you, Daryl. We're just going over the Gunningsville Bridge right now. The kids were spotted a few minutes ago, on the Moncton side of the river behind the hotel. We'll try to catch the boys there. If we miss them, we'll have to head them off somewhere along the marsh."

"You can't get Rescue 10 down onto the marsh," said Daryl. "There's no road."

"I know," came back Reg's voice. *"We'll have to leave the truck at the road and hike out to the river on foot."*

Daryl shook his head. All of Rescue 10's fancy equipment was useless if the truck couldn't get down to the river. If the firefighters had to walk, they would only be able to bring whatever rescue gear they could carry. And anything they carried was sure to slow them down.

Daryl swerved suddenly around a slow-moving car and leaned on his horn.

"Where's a siren when you need one?" he muttered.

Petra pulled her seatbelt a little tighter as Hobart leaned heavily against her for balance. Daryl glanced over at her.

"Sorry, Petra," he apologized with a wry grin. "Guess your birthday ski trip just turned into a fishing trip."

"That's okay," said Petra. "I'm going to be a firefighter too, someday. This will be good practice."

"Except that this isn't a practice, Petra. It's the real thing." Daryl's voice became serious. "You'll have to stay in the truck. Out of harm's way. Rescue work can be dangerous."

"But I can help, Uncle Daryl. Honest, I can!"

"I can't take chances with your safety, Petra," said her uncle sternly. He glanced sideways at his niece. Seeing her disappointed expression, his voice softened. "Just stay in the truck, okay? At least until I see how things are going. But if I do need help, you'll be the first to know. Deal?"

Petra hesitated. Then she nodded. "Deal."

She turned to look out the window. Her stomach tickled with excitement. At last, she was going on a real emergency call.

They were travelling down Riverview's main street now. Uncle Daryl weaved skilfully through traffic. From somewhere up ahead, Petra could hear sirens. Police sirens. Fire engine sirens. Another siren came screaming up from behind. Daryl pulled the truck to the side of the road just as an ambulance went roaring past. Daryl grabbed the com radio.

"Come in, Reg. This is Daryl. Did something happen?"

There was another hiss of static and Reg's voice answered: "*We missed them, Daryl.*"

"What happened?" Petra held her breath as they waited for Reg's reply.

"*An officer threw them a rope but it missed. They've been swept around the riverbend. We can't see them anymore. It's anybody's guess where they'll end up now. We're keeping the ambulance on stand-by, just in case.*"

"What's the plan?" asked Daryl.

"*We're going to keep following the Petitcodiac*

along the Moncton side of the river. Maybe we can catch up to them along the Dover Road somewhere."

"Good," said Daryl. "Petra and I will check out this side of the river. Maybe the current will bring them back over this way."

"*I've got Butch in the truck with me,*" said Reg. "*He has his diving gear.*"

Petra knew Butch. He was a tall, young firefighter with big ears and a bigger smile. He was also a professional diver, certified in water rescue missions.

"Good," said Daryl.

"*But Daryl…?*" Reg's voice hesitated.

"Go ahead, Reg."

"*It's not diving weather today.*"

Daryl was silent for a minute. He stared straight ahead out the windshield. His expression was grim. Then he took a deep breath and spoke into the radio.

"Roger that," he said. "Over and out."

"What did Reg mean by 'It's not diving weather'?" asked Petra in a small voice. She had seldom seen her fun-loving uncle look so serious.

"It means that he won't let Butch in the water today. The river is too cold and fast—even for a diver in a wetsuit. It's too dangerous." Daryl shook his head. "Anybody who goes into that water today isn't coming out again. There's nothing Butch can do."

"But…who's going to save the boys?" asked Petra.

For a moment, her uncle didn't answer.

"I should take you home," he said.

"No way!" said Petra. "I'm staying with you. Besides, it would take too long to bring me home. Every minute counts in an emergency, Uncle Daryl. That's what you always say."

"True enough," said Uncle Daryl with a small smile.

Petra glanced in the rearview mirror at the trailer rattling along behind them.

"We could use the boat," she said.

"We could," said her uncle, "if we could get it in the water. Which we can't. We need a launching ramp. The Zodiac isn't a canoe, you know. It's too heavy to lift and too heavy to carry down to the water's edge. And the road doesn't go to the river."

"No," said Petra, "but Mill Creek does."

Daryl turned in his seat. "Petra," he said, staring at her, "that just might work."

Mill Creek was a narrow, twisty ribbon of water that slipped down from the wooded hills above Riverview to pass underneath the highway just outside town before snaking across the marsh to join up with the Petitcodiac River. At low tide, Mill Creek was little more than a trickle at the bottom of a muddy trench. But if the tide was high enough, there might be just enough water to float a Zodiac raft. Maybe.

Daryl shifted gears. The engine growled. The truck leaped forward.

On the seat next to Petra, Hobart whined anxiously. Petra patted him.

"It's okay, Hobie. We're on a rescue mission. You can be our official fire-rescue dog. Try to think like a Dalmatian."

Hobart snorted and shook his heavy head, spraying the cab with dog drool.

Daryl laughed. "You know, Newfoundlands have probably saved more lives than Dalmatians."

"Really?"

"Sure. They used to dive into the ocean to rescue sailors and fishermen who had been swept overboard."

"Wow," said Petra, looking at the big dog with new-found respect.

"Of course, old Hobart here is a landlubber. The only thing he's used to diving into is his bowl of dog chow."

"Oh," said Petra.

Hobart burped softly and laid his head on Petra's shoulder.

"Here…" Daryl reached into the glove compartment and pulled out a pair of binoculars. "See if you can spot anything on the river."

They were approaching the edge of town now and far below the clusters of subdivision houses, Petra could see glimpses of the marsh. In summer, the marsh was a rippling, gold-green sea of grass that stood as tall as Petra's head. Now, in winter, the marsh looked like a white ocean, with snow drifts curling across its surface like great white waves frozen in time.

But beneath the snow and frozen grass, the marsh was swampy and treacherous. A person could get stuck in mud and silt washed up by the tides. Or break through the snowy crust into an unseen bog. Or find their way barred by one of the many muddy creeks that curled across the marsh like slippery brown eels.

Petra lowered the binoculars with a sigh. "Nothing. Do you think we've passed them?"

"I don't know." Her uncle shook his head. "Our only chance is to get ahead of them and get the boat to the river before they go past us."

"I wonder what they're thinking."

"Who?"

"The boys."

"I imagine they're pretty anxious to get off that piece of ice."

The Petitcodiac looks so different in the winter, thought Petra, looking at the river through the binoculars again. *It looks like a frozen slushy when it's still churning inside the machine at the ice cream store.*

She remembered her uncle's words about nobody being able to survive in water like that.

"I sure hope they don't try to swim for it," she said.

6

Point of No Return

"Maybe we should swim for it," said Tony.

"I don't know," said Shawn doubtfully.

"What other chance do we have?" said Tony. "We've gone around the bend. Nobody can reach us now. We should swim before the river gets any wider. The bank doesn't look that far."

Shawn squinted at the bank. It looked pretty far to him.

"I can't swim very well," shivered Craig. "I can't even feel my feet anymore."

The ice floe bobbed as a wave washed against it, sending another ripple of water across their boots. The boys braced themselves on the slick, wet ice, clutching each other's arms.

"We've got to do something," persisted Tony. "We can't stay on this thing. We'll freeze!"

"If we swim, we'll freeze *and* drown," said Shawn, bluntly. "The water's too cold. And look at those banks...we'd never be able to climb up them."

"If we stay on this ice floe, we're dead anyway," argued Tony. "We're either gonna freeze to death or get tipped into the river or float out to the ocean.

What other choice have we got? We've gone around the bend. It's the point of no return, guys! Don't you get it? Nobody is coming for us."

Shawn bit his lip.

"If we don't save ourselves, who will?" continued Tony. "We should at least try to reach shore."

The boys looked down at the chocolate-coloured water. Chunks of ice bobbed in the slushy brown liquid…it looked almost like the iced cappuccino that Shawn's mother sometimes drank.

"Our jackets and stuff would fill with water and drag us down," said Shawn.

"We'll take them off," said Tony, starting to tug at his zipper.

"Shawn, I can't swim that far!" said Craig.

"We'll help you, Craig," said Tony, "won't we, Shawn?"

Shawn hesitated. What should they do? What other chance did they have?

Slowly he started to pull down his jacket zipper. Tony was already shrugging his arms out of his sleeves. He dropped his jacket at his feet, in the puddle of water that now covered the top of the ice floe.

"O-k-k-k-kay," said Tony, his teeth already chattering as he stood shivering in just his sweatshirt, "W-w-we'll make f-f-for that chunk of m-m-m-mud sticking out from the b-b-b-bank over there."

"I don't think this is such a good idea, Tony," said Shawn.

Tony opened his mouth to argue, but just at that second, Craig hollered, "Look out!"

Tony and Shawn whipped around just in time to see what Craig was pointing at: a large, half-submerged tree trunk was bearing down on them like a giant prehistoric crocodile.

"It's going to hit us!" yelled Craig.

"Paddle!" shouted Shawn.

"What about frostbite?" yelped Tony.

"*Frostbite*?" said Shawn. "You were ready to go swimming a minute ago…now you're worried about frostbite?"

"Good point," said Tony.

"Everybody paddle!" said Shawn. "If that thing hits us, it'll smash the ice floe and then we really *will* be swimming!"

The boys dropped to their knees. The ice floe wobbled dangerously.

"Careful!" said Shawn. "Don't tip us over!"

They each stuck a hand in the water and paddled.

The water was so cold it burned. Tears stung Shawn's eyes.

Slowly, slowly the ice floe started to spin away from the tree trunk.

"K-k-keep…g-g-going," said Shawn through clenched teeth.

"I c-c-can't!" said Tony, "My hand! It hurts!"

"We can do it, Shawn!" said Craig. He dug his mitten into the water again. And again.

The tree was coming closer and closer. It was moving surprisingly fast. Too fast.

"It's going to hit us," moaned Shawn.

"Keep paddling!" said Craig. The brothers dipped their hands into the water again. The cold bit like teeth into their hands and arms—a stabbing pain that went right to the bone.

"Here it comes," said Shawn. He closed his eyes.

Craig dug into the water one more time, choking back a yelp of pain as the cold burned into his skin. The ice floe spun slightly. It was almost enough.

But not quite.

The branches at the very tip of the tree trunk scraped against the ice floe as it went sailing past. There was a grating noise; a crackling, crunching sound. A chunk of ice right next to Shawn's boot crumbled and floated away on the slushy, chocolate water.

"Ah!" yelled Shawn as his foot slipped off the ice floe. He went down hard on one knee, his other leg disappearing into the water. "Help!"

"I've got you, Shawn!" yelled Craig, hauling his big brother back up onto the ice floe. The boys stood shivering and stared at each other in shocked silence.

"Th-th-that was c-c-close," said Craig at last.

"Too close!" agreed Shawn. His pants were soaked up past his knee on his left leg.

Then the brothers noticed Tony. He was curled in a ball on the ice between them. The jacket that he had taken off was lying beneath him on the wet ice.

"Tony!" said Shawn. "Are you all right?"

Tony didn't answer.

Craig and Shawn crouched down beside him. Tony was shaking all over.

"Tony!" said Shawn again, shaking his friend's shoulder. "You've got to stand up...you're getting all wet!"

"T-t-too c-c-cold..." chattered Tony, his lips blue.

"Help me get him up, Craig," ordered Shawn. The boys grabbed their friend under each arm and started to pull.

"J-j-just l-l-l-et me r-r-rest here for a bit," mumbled Tony. "S-s-s-sleepy..."

"Don't go to sleep!" Shawn yelled at him. "Tony! Do you hear me? Wake up!" He turned to Craig. "He's starting to freeze. We've got to get him warmed up. We can't let him fall asleep or he might not wake up again!"

Craig bit his lip. He always did that when he was upset. "I wish Mom or Dad was here."

Shawn took a deep, shuddering breath. "Well, they're *not* here, so we just have to do the best we can." Standing on either side of their friend, the boys heaved Tony upright, but Tony just sagged between them.

The two brothers stared at each other as they struggled to hold Tony upright.

"So now what do we do?" asked Craig.

Up the Creek

"We've got to get this boat in the water!" said Daryl. The pickup truck and trailer had just squealed to a halt beneath the "Welcome to Riverview" sign at the town limits. Below them, Mill Creek flowed through a culvert under the road and gurgled on its way to join the Petitcodiac. Daryl ran to the trailer and began unhitching the raft.

Opening the passenger door, Petra hopped out of the truck. "Stay, Hobie," she said. She ran to the guardrail and looked over. "It's a long drop down to the creek," she observed.

"At least gravity will be on our side once we get this thing over the rail," said her uncle. He grunted, struggling to lift the raft.

"It's too heavy!" Daryl gasped. "I can't lift it by myself!"

Petra lifted the binoculars again. She looked upriver. Nothing. And then—"I see something!"

A small, dark shape could just be seen coming around the bend in the river.

"Let me see," Uncle Daryl took the binoculars.

"Is it them? Is it them?" Petra was full of anxiety.

"It's them." Daryl tossed the binoculars to Petra and dashed back to the raft. Once again he struggled to lift it.

"It's no good. We're going to miss them!" Daryl looked around frantically. Then he ran into the middle of the road. Waving his arms, he flagged down a car that was just coming over the hill. The car stopped.

A young man got out. "Engine trouble?" he asked.

"Boat trouble," said Uncle Daryl, pointing at the Zodiac.

The young man looked confused. "You're going boating here? Today?"

"I'm a firefighter," explained Daryl as he hurried the young man toward the Zodiac. "We have an emergency situation. Three boys are adrift on the river and I need to get to them. Can you help me lift the raft over the guardrail?"

"Sure thing!" said the man. He grabbed one side of the raft. Uncle Daryl grabbed the other.

"Ready?" asked Daryl. "On three. One. Two. Three. Heave!"

Grunting with effort, the two men hoisted the raft up off the trailer. For a split second, it hung in the air above the guardrail...

Then everything happened at once.

Hobart, excited by the sight of the airborne boat, leaped from the truck and let loose an explosive bark right in the ear of the young man.

Startled, the young man jumped. And lost his grip on the Zodiac.

The raft lurched sideways, knocking into Uncle Daryl. Caught off balance, Daryl slipped on the icy shoulder of the road. He went down hard, hooking his arm over the guardrail as he fell.

Down came the raft, on top of the guardrail. Right on top of Uncle Daryl's arm. Petra heard an awful cracking sound. But far worse was the sound her uncle made: a gut-wrenching groan of pain.

For one endless second, the raft teetered on the guardrail. Then it slipped over the edge, crashing and sliding down the bank to land with a squelch in the muddy creek.

Daryl crumpled onto the side of the road and lay very still.

"Uncle Daryl!" Petra screamed. She ran over and knelt beside him. His arm was bleeding. Through the torn fabric of his coat, Petra glimpsed the white gleam of bone.

The young man came running over and kneeled next to Petra. He turned a little green when he saw Uncle Daryl's arm. "Whoa…that's bad."

"Hang on, Uncle Daryl," Petra said. She ran to the truck. She grabbed the com radio.

"Rescue 10! Come in Rescue 10! This is Petra."

"*Well, howdy, Pretty Petra. This is Rescue 10. What's up?*" said Reg's friendly voice.

"Reg! Uncle Daryl's hurt! Come quick!"

"*Where are you?*" Reg's voice was suddenly brisk and serious.

"At Mill Creek. We were trying to put the raft in the water so we could rescue the boys, but Uncle Daryl slipped and I think his arm is broken…"

"*All right. Just sit tight, Petra. We're on our way.*"

"But Reg…the boys on the ice floe—they're almost here."

There was silence on the radio for a moment. Then Reg said, "*Just keep your uncle comfortable. We'll be there as soon as we can.*"

"But what about the boys? What should I do?"

"*Nothing. There's nothing you can do. Just wait for us.*"

Petra clicked off the radio.

She grabbed the heavy blanket that Daryl always kept in the back seat. She ran back to her uncle and spread the blanket over him. The young man had wadded up his jacket and placed it under Daryl's head.

"I just radioed for help," Petra told the young man. "Don't try to move him or anything."

Petra stood up and looked out at the river. There they were! The boys on the ice floe. They were getting closer. She could see three figures huddled together. Two were standing. The third was sort of slumped between them.

In the distance, Petra could hear sirens. Rescue 10 was coming fast.

So was the ice floe. And the ice floe was closer.

Petra made up her mind. She hopped the guardrail and slid down the bank.

"Hey!" the young man shouted after her. "What are you doing?"

"Something!" Petra yelled back.

The raft was half-in, half-out of the water. She gave it a shove. The rubber boat slid easily on the icy slope. Down into the creek it went with a wet *splat*. Petra hopped in. She pulled the cord on the motor. *Just like starting the lawnmower at home*, she told herself.

R-rrrrrr! R-rrrrrr!

"Come on!" Petra gritted her teeth and yanked the cord again.

R-R-R-RRRRRRRRRRRRRRRRRRRRRR!

The motor snarled to life. Petra sat down and put her hand on the tiller. Just then something big and black came barrelling down the bank and launched itself at the boat.

"Hobart!"

The raft rocked crazily as the big dog leaped aboard.

"Hobart! Go back! Go back to the truck!"

Hobart gave a loud bark. He ran to the bow of the boat and stood looking toward the river. He barked again and looked over his shoulder at Petra.

In spite of everything, Petra had to smile. "Aye, aye, Captain," she said, "anchors aweigh!"

She eased open the throttle and the raft moved slowly forward through the murky water. The creek was so narrow that the sides of the Zodiac scraped against the muddy sides.

"Come on, come on," breathed Petra. The Zodiac *putt-putted* down the creek. She looked ahead. Where was the ice floe? Mill Creek was too low, its banks too high. She couldn't see the Petitcodiac River from down here. She eased the Zodiac around another tight turn — Mill Creek was shaped like a squashed letter *S*. Petra held her breath as the Zodiac squeezed between the banks. It was a tight fit. She hoped the boat wouldn't get stuck.

The motor sputtered as the propeller churned its way through mud and marsh grass. Petra opened the throttle. The motor caught again, and the Zodiac surged around the last bend in the creek.

The Petitcodiac River was just ahead!

Petra opened the throttle as far as it would go. The Zodiac shot out of the creek like a cork popping out of a bottle. They were out on the open water of the Petitcodiac River! The wind whipped Petra's hair around her face. Hobart's long black ears flapped around his head like sails. The fast-moving current immediately hit the raft, trying to push it downriver. Petra gunned the engine and struggled to hold the tiller steady. She looked up and down the river.

Where was the ice floe? Where were the boys? Had she missed them? Had they already gone by?

Petra looked back toward the highway. Way up on the road, she could see flashing red lights. Rescue

10 had arrived. She saw firefighters bending over Uncle Daryl. She saw the young man pointing in her direction. Some of the firefighters began running across the marsh toward her. From this distance, they looked like little action figures.

Petra turned her attention back to the river. She knew there was nothing they could do. There was no time left. It was up to her now. She shielded her eyes with her hand and looked out over the brown water.

There they were!

Petra saw the ice floe. It was moving swiftly, way out in the middle of the river. She pulled hard on the rudder, steering the boat diagonally across the current. The waves slapped angrily against the hull, trying to bully the raft off-course. Petra gripped the rudder more tightly. She squinted again at the boys' ice floe, trying to gauge its speed and distance. Yes, if she could just hold this course, she should be able to intercept the ice floe a few metres downstream. But she would have to hurry.

Petra opened the throttle on the Zodiac's motor. The motor sputtered. Choked.

And died.

8

That Sinking Feeling

"Tony, wake up!" cried Shawn. "You've got to stand up! We can't hold you!"

Tony was slipping out of the brothers' grasp. As they struggled to hold him, the ice floe teetered beneath their feet.

"We've got to warm him up!" said Craig. "Can you reach his jacket?"

"It's wet!" said Shawn.

"Is it better to have a wet jacket or no jacket at all?" wondered Craig.

"I don't know," said Shawn in despair. It was like a riddle with no answer. He let go of Tony with one hand and groped for the jacket by his feet. He picked it up. "I don't think it's soaked all the way through," he said, "just in some places. Let's put it back on him."

Moving carefully, Craig and Shawn manoeuvred Tony's arms back into the sleeves of his coat.

"I c-c-can't get the zipper," said Craig, "my fingers are too cold."

"Mine too," said Shawn. "Wait, I have an idea." He unwrapped his scarf from his neck. He pulled Tony's jacket closed and tied the scarf around Tony's waist. The jacket stayed closed, sort of.

"That'll have to do for now," said Shawn. He pulled Tony's hood up over his head. "What else can we do to warm him up?"

"Rub his arms," said Craig. "That's what Mom does to me when I get too cold at the beach."

"Right," said Shawn. They both started rubbing Tony's arms vigorously. Tony groaned.

"Come on, Tony," said Shawn, "wake up!"

Tony lifted his head. He blinked and looked around him. He squeezed his eyes shut and opened them again. He groaned. "Oh man," Tony mumbled, "I thought I was just having a nightmare…but we're still on the ice floe!"

"This is no nightmare," said Shawn. "It's worse."

"My mittens are soaked, Shawn," said Craig. "I can hardly feel my fingers."

"Mine too," said Shawn.

"I don't want my fingers to get frostbite and fall off!" said Craig.

"Calm down," said Shawn, "we just have to dry them off."

"W-w-with what?" said Tony.

Shawn had an idea. "Our hats are dry," he said.

The boys peeled off their soaked mittens. They took off their hats and pulled their hoods back over their heads. Then they dried their fingers with their hats.

They huddled together for warmth, wearing their hats on their hands.

"So I g-g-guess swimming is out of the question," shivered Tony with a feeble grin.

"Yup, I think we can scratch that idea," said Shawn. "We're too far from shore now anyway."

He was right. The river had gotten bigger. Much, much bigger. Now they were drifting in the middle of a wide channel of deep brown water. Water that was flowing faster and faster on its way to the sea.

Craig noticed something else.

"Um, guys?" he asked.

"What is it?" said Shawn, rubbing his hands briskly together inside his hat as he tried to warm his fingers.

"Have you noticed there's a lot less ice in the river now?"

Shawn and Tony lifted their heads and looked around. Craig was right. Before, the river had been choked with chunks of ice and snow and frozen mud. Now, only a few other ice floes dotted the growing expanse of open water.

"What's happening to all the ice?" asked Craig uneasily.

A medium-sized ice floe floating beside them caught their eye. As the boys watched, a wave washed over it. When the wave was gone, so was the piece of ice. Only some scattered hunks of slush remained, bobbing among the chocolate waves.

"Where did it go?" asked Tony. Fear made his voice sound tight and squeaky.

"It's breaking up," said Shawn. "The water is getting faster and deeper. So there's not as much ice."

"It's melting," whispered Craig. "All the ice is melting."

The boys looked down at their feet. The puddle was getting bigger. The ice floe was getting smaller.

"We have got to get off this thing," said Shawn, "or we're sunk."

Out of Time

"No, no, no!" said Petra, yanking at the starter cord on the Zodiac's motor. "Don't do this! Not now!"

But the motor refused to catch. Petra peered over the side of the boat into the water. Long strands of marsh grass streamed out from beneath the motor. They were tangled in a gummy knot around the propeller.

Hobart barked. Petra sat back up. Hobart barked again. He could see the boys on the ice floe. He looked at Petra and whined. Petra looked around, then grabbed one of the two oars in the bottom of the boat. Leaning over the side of the boat, she stabbed the oar at the propeller, trying to pry away some of the muddy grass.

"Come on!" she grunted, giving the motor another whack with the oar. A few clumps of mud broke free and sank out of sight. Petra dropped the oar into the bottom of the boat and yanked again on the starter cord.

Rrrrrrrrr! The raft surged forward again, bouncing across the waves. She was almost there. Another minute and she'd be able to pull up alongside the ice floe.

Rrrr-ka-chuff! The motor coughed, jerked, and stopped.

"Not again!" said Petra. She grabbed the oar and scraped at the knot of grass still wrapped around the propeller. It was no use. Short of diving into the water and cutting the grass with a knife, there was no way to loosen the long, strangling strands.

"Guess we'll have to do this the old-fashioned way, Hobie," Petra said. She fitted the oars in the oarlocks and braced her feet against the bottom of the boat.

Down went the oars into the water. Petra pulled, reached forward, and pulled again. And again.

Slowly, slowly, the raft started to move across the current. Brown waves slapped against its side, spraying Petra and Hobart with freezing water. Reach-pull, reach-pull…the muscles in her arms were burning in spite of the cold. Still, Petra rowed for all she was worth. If the ice floe got past her, there would be no catching it. Not in this current. Not without a motor.

Breathing hard, Petra paused to shake her wet hair out of her eyes and get her bearings. She looked upriver and spotted the ice floe. She was almost there.

She wondered if the boys had seen her yet. *Do they know that someone's trying to help them?* Petra blinked the water out of her eyes and squinted toward the figures huddled on the ice floe. They appeared to be speaking urgently to one another. Petra wondered what they could be talking about on that little piece of floating ice.

"We're losing ice!" said Craig.

It was true. Almost every wave that rippled over the floe carried away another piece of the crumbling ice. Tony half-turned his body to look toward the shore. The ice floe tilted dangerously. A large wave sloshed onto the ice, soaking the boys up to their ankles.

"Whoa!!" yelled all three boys. Slowly, slowly the ice floe righted itself again.

"Do *not* move!" ordered Shawn.

"Move?" croaked Tony, "Man, I'm barely breathing!"

Another wave washed the ice floe. A piece of the ice crumbled away.

"It's breaking apart, Shawn," whispered Craig. His blue eyes were very wide.

"Don't move," repeated Shawn.

"We're out of time," Tony said softly. "This is it."

"Boat," whispered Craig hoarsely, his lips blue and numb with cold.

"I know we need a boat, Craig," said Shawn, "but we don't have one."

"Boat!" said Craig again.

"Craig, I know you want a boat," said Shawn. "We all want a boat, but… "

"No, no…*boat*!" shouted Craig, and he pointed.

The other two boys slowly turned to look.

"Holy cow! It's a boat!" said Tony, wonderingly. "Shawn, it's a boat!"

The boys watched as a rubber raft bobbed and pitched on the waves across the river. It seemed to be moving slowly toward them.

"Shawn?" said Tony.

"Yeah?"

"Does hypothermia make a person hallucinate?"

"I don't know. Why?"

"Because it looks like there's a bear driving that boat."

"Yeah," breathed Craig. "I see it too!"

"Maybe it's a mirage," said Shawn. "Like when people think they see water when they're hot and thirsty and lost in the desert. Except we're seeing a boat because we're cold and wet and lost on the water."

"That's weird," said Tony.

"Well, it's been kind of a weird day," Craig pointed out.

"True," said Tony.

They all watched the raft in silence for a moment. Another wave sloshed over the ice floe.

"So...did we decide if the bear is real or not?" asked Tony. "Because I was just wondering: is it better to freeze to death on an ice floe or get eaten by a bear?"

"It's probably warmer inside the bear," said Craig thoughtfully.

"Good point," said Tony. He waved his arms at the raft: "Hey! Yoo-hooo! Bear! Over here!"

The bear barked.

"Hypothermia has some weird side effects," remarked Tony.

"That's no bear," said Shawn, looking hard at the boat.

"Oh." Tony sounded slightly disappointed. "Then I guess the boat's not real either?" He sighed.

"No, the boat's real, all right," said Shawn. His voice was rising with excitement. He grabbed Tony's shoulder and pointed. "Look! It's not a bear...it's a dog! We're going to be rescued!"

"By a bear-sized, boat-driving dog? Uh, Shawn—I think the hypothermia's getting to you, too."

"No, dork! We're gonna be rescued by the person who's *with* the dog."

"Must be a smart dog if it can drive a boat."

"Tony, he's not driving the boat!"

"Oh. Well, that's good news."

The three boys stood in silence, watching the small raft fight its way through the waves. It seemed to move very slowly.

Another small piece broke off the ice floe. The boys watched as it floated away.

"So," began Tony again, "Is it better to freeze to death on a sinking ice floe or be eaten by a bear-sized dog?"

"Forget the dog, Tony."

"I was just making conversation."

"Well, don't."

"Uh, guys?" interrupted Craig.

"*What?*" said Shawn and Tony together.

Craig was looking at the boat. "I don't think the boat is going to make it in time. It's not going fast enough. We're going to pass it before it reaches us."

Another chip of ice crumbled away into the water.

"Uh-uh," said Tony. "We're going to *sink* before it reaches us."

"Either way, the situation is not good," said Shawn. "Not good at all. We've got to do something."

All Aboard!

"Hobie, we've got to do something!" gasped Petra.

The Zodiac was almost at the ice floe—almost, but not quite. The ice floe was starting to slip past the raft.

"Hey!" shouted Petra, waving her arms at the boys. "Hey, there!"

"Help us!" shouted the tallest boy.

"We're sinking!" shouted the shortest boy.

"Has your dog eaten recently?" shouted the middle-sized boy.

"Just hang on!" shouted Petra.

The middle-sized boy spread out his empty hands and shrugged. "To what?"

"To this," said Petra.

She picked up the coil of mooring rope lying on the bottom of the boat. She stood up and began swinging the rope above her head.

"Oh no," groaned Tony, "not the rope trick again."

"She's closer than the police officer was," said Shawn. "We'll catch it this time."

"We have to," added Craig.

Petra let go of the rope.

Four young people held their breath as it uncoiled through the air and landed with a wet slap—on the ice floe.

All three boys pounced on the rope as it began sliding back toward the water. The ice floe rocked violently. Craig slipped and went down hard on his chest.

"*Oof!*"

One arm plunged into the river and his head and shoulders hung out over the edge of the ice floe. A brown wave lapped against his chin.

"Shawn!"

And then his brother was grabbing him under the armpits, hauling him back to his feet.

The ice floe had an alarming tilt now. It was tipping the boys toward the edge. Three pairs of boots began sliding toward the deep, swirling, brown water.

"Quick!" hollered Shawn. He pulled on the rope. So did Petra. The ice floe and the boat came together with a gentle bump. The floe tilted even more.

"Grab hold of this!" said Petra, extending one of the oars toward the boys.

"Got it!" said Craig, grabbing for the oar.

"Got it!" said Tony, lunging for the oar at exactly the same moment.

The sudden weight of the two boys wrenched the oar from Petra's grasp.

"Hey!" she protested, "Watch it!"

The ice floe lurched.

"Yikes!"

Tony and Craig dropped the oar and grabbed onto each other for support as the back of the ice floe lifted completely out of the water.

"Jump!" said Tony. They did, all three tumbling over the rubber sides of the raft into the bottom of the boat.

Slowly the boys sat up. They looked over the side of the boat.

An expanse of chocolate waves flickered and winked at them in the sunlight. A few scattered pieces of ice gleamed on the brown surface, bobbing helter-skelter like debris from a wreckage.

"Glad you could drop in," said a voice behind them. The three boys turned. The tall, rosy-cheeked girl had taken off her hat and was shaking the water out of her hair. She yanked the hat back down over her ears and held up her hand in greeting: "I'm Petra."

"Shawn," said Shawn. "And this is Craig, my brother. And that's Tony."

"N-n-nice doggy," said Tony as the big Newfoundland leaned against him, drooling gently on his shoulder.

Petra laughed. "That's Hobart. He's about as fierce as a baby chicken."

"Thanks for coming to get us," said Shawn.

"I would've got here sooner," said Petra, "but I had a bit of engine trouble." She suddenly looked worried.

"So, uh, where are the other rescuers?" Shawn asked, hoping this didn't sound impolite.

"My uncle had an accident," said Petra shortly. "The other firefighters were on their way, but I was the first on the scene. So I acted. It's what firefighters are supposed to do," she added defensively.

"I'm glad you didn't wait," said Craig. "Five more seconds and we would have been Chocolate River popsicles."

"So, can we go home now?" asked Tony. "I don't know about you guys, but I am wet and f-f-freezing!"

"Um…" said Petra.

The three boys looked at her.

"We have a bit of a problem," she said.

Adrift

"What do you mean the motor's broken?" exclaimed Tony in disbelief. "What kind of a rescue is this, anyway?"

"Well, if you don't like it, you can always hop on another ice floe and wait for the next rescue raft to come along!" retorted Petra hotly.

"No, no," said Shawn hastily, stepping between them. "That's all right. This rescue raft is great. Much, much better than the ice floe. Right, Tony?" Shawn gave his friend a sharp jab with his elbow.

"Huh? Oh, yeah. I guess," said Tony, slumping against the side of the raft.

Hobart gave a low *woof!* in Tony's ear. Tony shot up very straight. "I mean, yes! For sure! This is absolutely the best rescue raft I've ever been on."

Hobart snorted and laid his head back down on his paws.

"It would be even better if we had a rescue raft that worked," Tony whispered to Craig.

"Can't we just paddle back the way you c-c-c-came?" asked Craig. He had started to shiver uncontrollably again. Petra shook her head.

"Kind of hard to row with one oar," Petra pointed out, holding up the one remaining paddle.

"Oh yeah," said Tony, sheepishly. "Sorry about that."

"It's too late, anyway," Petra said. "We'd never be able to row back upriver against this current. Look how far we've come." She pointed.

The entrance to Mill Creek was far behind them. The swift current had already pushed the disabled raft many metres downstream. The banks sliding past them now were high and rocky, bristling at the top with prickly evergreen trees. Rescue 10 and the firefighters could no longer be seen. Neither could the road. Petra shook her head.

"We'll just have to ride it out and try to find another place to land the boat."

"Hopefully b-b-before we reach the ocean," said Craig.

Petra smiled, but her eyes were worried. "Yeah, hopefully," she told the younger boy.

It was now late afternoon and the mid-winter sun was already hanging low in the sky. The horizon was golden-pink. At this time of the year, it got dark by suppertime.

Shawn shivered and wiggled his toes inside his wet boots. His mitts were soaked too. So were the knees of his ski pants. He looked over at the other boys. Tony was huddled in a ball with his arms wrapped around his knees. Craig was slumped against the side of the raft. Shivers racked his body. His face was pale and his lips were blue. As Shawn watched, Craig's eyes began to close.

"Craig!" said his brother sharply. "Wake up!"

Craig's eyes fluttered open but almost immediately began to close again.

Quickly, Petra knelt beside him. She bent her head close to Craig's face and held very still, as if she was listening for something.

"What're you doing?" asked Shawn, worried.

"I'm checking his breathing," said Petra. "If a person gets hypothermia, their breathing can slow down. And even stop."

A cold metal fist seemed to clutch Shawn's heart. He dropped to his knees beside Petra. "How's Craig's breathing? Is he all right?" Shawn had never seen his little brother look so still and quiet.

"His breathing is okay so far," she said, sitting up. "But we have to get him warm. Tony, too," she added, nodding at the other boy's huddled form.

"Craig got wet," said Shawn miserably. "He slipped and his arm went into the water up to his shoulder."

"We need to get his wet clothes off," said Petra. "And we need to get him out of the wind." She began rummaging in the pack strapped around her waist.

"How are we going to get him out of the wind in an open raft in the middle of a river?" asked Shawn.

"With this," said Petra, handing him something in a small, plastic wrapper. The package was smaller than a CD. Shawn took it and examined it. Inside the wrapper was something that looked like a small, folded piece of tin foil.

"What is it?" asked Shawn.

"It's a space blanket."

"A what?"

"A space blanket," said Petra. "From my first aid kit."

"It looks like the inside of a chocolate bar wrapper," said Shawn, holding the tiny piece of foil in the palm of his hand. "How is this going to help us?"

"It's really light plastic sprayed with aluminum," explained Petra. "It's waterproof and windproof and it reflects your body heat back at you." She shook open the foil to reveal a thin but surprisingly big silver sheet. "So it's kind of like a self-warming blanket."

"Cool," said Shawn.

"It should be," said Petra. "It was invented by NASA."

"How do you know all this?" asked Shawn. "About hypothermia and space blankets and stuff, I mean?"

"First aid course," said Petra with a shrug. "I'm going to be a paramedic. Or maybe a firefighter. I haven't really decided yet."

"Oh," said Shawn. He thought about telling her that he wanted to build stuff when he grew up, like roller coasters and gadgets. But those things didn't seem very useful out in the middle of the Petitcodiac River. So instead he said, "What should I do?"

"We need to build some kind of shelter." Petra held up the space blanket and looked at it quizzically.

"Did you say 'build'?" said Shawn. He grinned and held out his hand. "Give me that, and show me what else you have in that pack of yours."

Ten minutes later, what looked like a small tinfoil tent crackled and snapped in the breeze. It was secured with white surgical tape from Petra's first aid kit and supported by the paddle, which Shawn had used as a centre pole. A boot lace (Shawn's) threaded through small holes (cut very carefully with a small pair of scissors from the first aid kit and reinforced with more surgical tape) kept the edges of the blanket from flapping open. A big, triangular cloth bandage (which Petra said was for making slings) was tied to the paddle, and hung down over the front of the tent like a door.

Inside lay Craig and Tony. Their feet stuck out a bit, but at least they were mostly protected from the wind and the spray from the river.

"Okay," said Shawn, rubbing his cold hands together. "What's next?"

"We have to get any wet clothes off them," said Petra.

"Craig's jacket is soaked all the way up the arm," said Shawn. "His shirt will be wet underneath it, too. But we can't take both his shirt and jacket off—he'll freeze to death! It's February!"

"He'll freeze faster with them on," said Petra shortly. "The water from the wet clothes takes heat from his body. We'll have to find something else to cover him up with."

"I sure hope you know what you're talking about," said Shawn, shaking his head. But he ducked into the tent and began taking off his brother's jacket. Petra touched Tony's sleeve.

"Tony's jacket is wet too," she said.

"Yeah," said Shawn. "It fell in a puddle."

Petra started to take off Tony's jacket.

"Hey…whatchyadoin? Gerroff me!" muttered Tony weakly, pushing Petra away.

"Relax, buddy," Shawn told him. "We're just going to find you something dry to wear."

"Whatever…" Tony mumbled through numb lips. His head sagged back against the raft. His eyes closed again. Petra got the jacket the rest of the way off.

Shawn eased Craig's soaking undershirt over his head. The small boy lay motionless in the bottom of the raft, looking thin and frail. His bare skin had a weird, pale glow beneath the silvery reflection of the space blanket. Shawn felt tears prickle behind his eyes as he looked at his brother. He had never been to a funeral, but Shawn had an awful suspicion that death looked a lot like this.

"So what do we do now? Shouldn't we rub his arms or something to warm him up?" Desperation edged Shawn's voice. But Petra shook her head.

"No. You can't rub a person with hypothermia; their body's in shock. You have to be careful." She dug through her pack again and pulled out four small packets, roughly the size of tea bags. "Thermal heating pads," she said, tossing them to Shawn. "I put them in my mittens to keep my hands warm when I'm skiing."

"They're so small," said Shawn. "What good are they?"

Petra shrugged. "They're better than nothing. There's two for each of them," she said, nodding at Tony and Craig. "Maybe if we put one on each of their necks and chests we can heat up their blood and it can spread to the rest of their bodies."

Shawn picked up his scarf from where it lay bundled up with Tony's cast-off jacket. He wrapped it loosely around Craig's neck and tucked a heating pad inside. He put the second heating pad right over Craig's heart. Shawn then shrugged quickly out of his own jacket and draped it over his brother like a blanket. Beside him, Petra was doing the same for Tony.

When she was done, she rocked back on her heels and surveyed her patients.

"Well, it's a start," she said. "But I wish we had something else to put over them."

A big black head poked through the flap of the silver tent. Hobart snuffled at the two boys lying cold and still inside. Then, before Petra could say anything, the big, shaggy dog pushed his way past her. Wriggling in on his belly, Hobart flopped down on top of the two boys with a loud, contented sigh, looking for all the world like a big bear-skin rug.

Petra raised her eyebrows. "That'll work," she said.

She let the tent flap fall closed and went and sat down next to Shawn. The river gurgled and slapped against the rubber sides of the raft. In silence they watched the landscape slide by. The treed cliffs had once more given way to sprawling marshes. Beyond the marsh, the land seemed to shrug its shoulders before stretching upward into sloping fields. And running along the very top of the fields, just where land met sky, was the road.

The sky was a deep denim blue now. Shawn could see headlights winking along the distant highway underneath the edge of the sky. People were heading home for dinner. Shawn thought of his mom and dad in their warm, cheery kitchen at home, getting supper ready. His throat closed. He swallowed hard. And shivered.

"Are you all right?" Petra was looking at him in concern.

Shawn rubbed his hand quickly across his eyes. "Yeah. Sure. I'm fine."

"You're cold," Petra stated. She started to take off the fleece vest she was wearing over her sweater.

"I'm okay," protested Shawn. But his teeth had started to chatter.

Petra held out the vest. "Take it," she said. "I've got lots of layers on, for skiing. It might be small, though."

Shawn nodded and took the vest. He was too cold to argue. "Thanks," he said.

"It's getting dark," observed Petra.

Shawn nodded again. Night was falling fast. He wondered if the rescuers would continue to look for them in the dark. "Do you have a flashlight in that pack of yours?" he asked.

Petra shook her head.

"A candle?" asked Shawn hopefully.

"Nope." She reached into her pack and brought out a small cardboard box. "Just these."

"What are they?" asked Shawn.

Petra opened the box and shook something into her hand. "Six...no, seven waterproof matches. If we were lost in the woods, I could build us a fire." She smiled lamely. "But there's nothing to burn here."

The last rays of sunlight clawed briefly at the skyline, then slipped below the horizon. A deep indigo curtain seemed to fall across the sky.

"We're in trouble," said Shawn.

Battle Against the Dark

During the New Brunswick winter, night strikes like a predator.

It's not like in the summer, when the evening sun stretches and arches its back across the sky with the lazy, unhurried grace of a cat preparing for a nap.

No.

In winter, day ends with a panic of colour that scrabbles across the sky before night pounces, pinning it down against the horizon. There is a last blood-red flicker…then daylight is gone, swallowed up by the night in a single gulp.

"Wow, it's dark," said Petra to Shawn.

"I know," said Shawn. "How far down the river do you think we are?"

"No idea," said Petra.

The cold pressed itself against them.

Below the boat, the river snickered and chuckled. The moon played an annoying game of peek-a-boo— sometimes splashing them with a weird silver light that lit up their faces like ghosts, and sometimes dousing them with darkness by disappearing behind the clouds.

Petra got up and kneeled by the space-blanket tent. She leaned inside. Shawn heard the *thump-thump* of Hobart's tail.

Shawn pulled aside the door flap and stuck his head in beside her.

"How are they doing?" he asked.

"A little better. I think," said Petra. "Hobart's body heat is helping a lot."

Shawn patted Craig's cheek. "How are you doing, bro?"

"We home yet?" mumbled Craig.

"Soon," Shawn told him. "It shouldn't be long now. You just hold on, okay?"

"'Kay," said Craig drowsily.

Shawn turned to Tony and gently shook his shoulder. "Hey, man…still there?"

Tony groaned. "Bad dream," he moaned. "Dreamed a bear sat on me." He opened one eye.

And saw a mountain of black fur draped across his chest. "*Ahhhh!* Not a dream! Help! Somebody save me! I'm being flattened by a bear!"

"Shhhhh!" said Shawn, trying not to laugh. "Not a bear. Just a dog. Dog, Tony! And he's not squashing you…he's just keeping you warm."

Hobart gave Tony a long, slobbery lick on the side of his face.

"Oh man!" wailed Tony. "Now he's checking to see what flavour I am!"

Petra tapped Shawn's shoulder. "Here," she said.

"See if they'll eat a little of this." She offered him a small plastic bag.

Shawn took the bag and peered inside.

"It's trail mix," said Petra, in a low voice. "Peanuts, raisins, dried fruit, and granola, a few chocolate chips. It's a good energy booster. I know it's not much." Petra sounded apologetic. "But it might help them fight off the cold a bit better."

"That's great—thanks." said Shawn. He was suddenly aware of how empty his own belly felt. It was past suppertime now. He shook a handful of the trail mix into his palm and passed it to Craig.

"Eat," he said. "You'll feel better."

While Craig munched, Shawn poured some trail mix into Tony's hand.

"What is it?" asked Tony suspiciously.

"Don't ask—eat!" said Shawn, who knew that Tony was a fussy eater, particularly when it came to nuts. He wasn't allergic to them; he just didn't like the way they felt between his teeth when he crunched them.

Tony chewed carefully. He swallowed. Then he gobbled down the rest and held out his hand for more.

"That's fantastic," he said. "What is this stuff?"

"Trail mix," said Shawn. "I thought you didn't like peanuts."

"Hate 'em," said Tony cheerfully as he scarfed down another fistful. "But they taste a whole lot different after you've been marooned on a sinking ice floe and stranded aboard a broken boat all day long."

The food seemed to revive the two boys. Craig struggled to sit up. The coat Shawn had tucked around him slid off. His bare chest glowed whitely in the dark. Craig snatched the jacket back up to his chin. He shot his brother a furious look.

"Why am I naked?" he hissed.

The darkness inside the tent hid Shawn's grin. "Relax. You're not naked. We just had to take your shirt off because it was wet."

"We?" said Craig. "*We*? You mean *she* saw me naked too? A girl? Shawn!"

"Will you shut up?" said Shawn. "Petra probably saved your life. She knows a lot. Anyway, how is it any different from when you go swimming? There are girls there too, you know."

"It's different," grumped Craig. "Trust me."

"Well, here. Take this then." Shawn unzipped the vest Petra had given him and passed it to Craig. Craig quickly put it on.

"Put on my coat, too," ordered Shawn. "Yours is still wet."

Craig did. "What about you?" he asked.

"I'm all right," said Shawn. "Stay here in the tent with Hobart and Tony. I'm going to see if I can figure out where we are."

He ducked back outside. Petra was standing in the bow of the raft, staring out over the river.

"See anything?" asked Shawn.

Petra shook her head. "Not much. The tide's getting lower, though," she added.

"How can you tell?"

"Because the banks are getting higher." Petra pointed.

The moon ducked out from behind a cloud, and in its teasing light, Shawn could see the sheer muddy walls looming high above them. They were down in the bottom of a deep chocolate trench. Along the top of the banks, boulder-sized chunks of ice were stacked crazily on top of each other, tossed there by the wild winter tides. Frozen together, their sharp edges bared at the moon, the blocks formed a fiercely jagged ridge of ice.

"It looks like the river has teeth," Shawn murmured, half to himself.

"Tell me about it," agreed Petra. "There's no climbing that, even if we could get the boat to shore."

She turned and started to sit back down...but suddenly stiffened, staring back at the river behind them.

"Look!" she breathed.

Off to their left, on the black stretch of marsh they had just passed, a parade of tiny lights were winking and winding their way through the darkness.

"What is it?" asked Shawn. But he already knew.

"It's the searchers!" cried Petra. "They're walking across the marsh to the river!"

Emotion grabbed Shawn by the throat. He didn't know if it was hope or despair that seemed to choke the air from his lungs.

"They're in the wrong place," he croaked. "We're already past them."

"Hey!" screamed Petra, waving her arms frantically. "Hey! We're over here! This way! Uncle Daryl, I'm over here!"

Her calls were swallowed up by the darkness. The lights didn't change course, but gathered instead at a point on the riverbank far behind them.

"No!" wailed Petra in sudden frustration. "No, no, no!" She aimed a savage kick at the side of the rubber raft. "Stupid boat! Stupid river! Stupid...*everything*." She dropped down onto the seat of the Zodiac and buried her face in her hands.

Shawn stood frozen in place. His blood hammered in his ears. *This is crazy. This can't be happening to us!* The thought ran over and over through his mind like a broken record. He took a deep, shaky breath. Then another one. He sat down next to Petra.

"Hey," he said softly.

"What?" she said, her face still hidden in her hands. Her voice sounded funny.

"We'll get off this boat somehow," said Shawn.

"*Sure* we will," said Petra. But she sniffed, and sat up straighter, rubbing her hand across her eyes.

"We just have to figure out a way for them to see us," he said, in what he hoped was an encouraging voice.

"Oh, sure. No problem," said Petra sarcastically. "Do you have a plan, Einstein?"

"Well, we need a candle, for starters," said Shawn.

"Can't help you," said Petra. "I'm fresh out of candles."

But Shawn had picked up Petra's fanny pack from the bottom of the raft and was digging though it again. "What's this?" he asked, holding up a small round metal canister.

Petra took it from him and looked at it. "Ski wax," she said, tossing it back to him. "Useful if you happen to be skiing on wet, sticky snow. Not useful if you're adrift on a river."

"I don't know about that…" Shawn was holding up the small tin of wax and looking at it thoughtfully. "What are candles made of?"

Petra suddenly sat up very straight.

"Wax!"

"Yup," said Shawn with a grin.

"Can you really make a candle out of that?" asked Petra. Hope had crept back into her voice.

"I can try. We need a wick, though. Like a piece of string or something. Something for the flame to burn along inside the wax."

Petra unwound her scarf and pulled at the fringe on the end. A long, thin strand of green yarn came away in her fingers. She broke it off and handed it to Shawn.

"Would this work?"

"Maybe. We just have to get the wick inside the wax."

"Well, how do candlemakers do it?"

Shawn shook his head. "They dip the wick in melted wax over and over until it gets a thick coating. It takes a long time. You have to let the wax harden between each coat."

"How are we going to do that?" asked Petra, discouraged. "We can't melt this whole can."

"I know," said Shawn, examining the wax, "but I think if we can make a small enough hole in the middle of the wax, we can feed the wick down the hole to the bottom of the can. Then we can just melt enough wax to fill in the hole around the wick."

"What are you going to use to make the hole?" asked Petra.

"I don't know," admitted Shawn. "Do you have any sewing needles in that kit?"

"I don't sew," stated Petra. "I ski."

Shawn sighed. "Do we have anything else sharp?"

"Those scissors we used on the blanket," said Petra.

Shawn shook his head. "The blade's too wide. We'd just end up hacking up the ski wax. A piece of wire might work." He ran his fingers through his hair in exasperation. "There must be *something* on this raft that we can use. Look in the first aid kit again."

Petra looked. "There's nothing in here but band-aids. And stingy stuff for cuts. And, uh…more cloth bandages. And—oh, hold on! Here's something!" She held up a small plastic package of safety pins.

"Perfect!" said Shawn.

He took a safety pin and bent it back so it became

one long piece of wire with a sharp end. He pressed it straight down into the canister of ski wax. He pulled the pin out.

"Hand me the yarn," he said.

Petra did. Shawn speared the end of the yarn with the pin and then pressed the pin back down into the wax. He eased the pin out of the hole. The yarn stayed in the wax.

"Got a match?" asked Shawn.

"Right here," said Petra.

"Light it and hold it over the canister," instructed Shawn.

Petra struck the match, cupping her hand around the flame to keep the wind from blowing it out. Shawn held the can of ski wax with the green yarn up to the match. He rotated it slowly. The wax began to melt onto the yarn, filling in the hole.

"Ow!" said Petra suddenly. The match went out.

"What happened?"

"Burnt my finger," said Petra's voice in the sudden dark. "Those matches don't last very long."

"Pass me the scissors," said Shawn. "I'm going to trim the wick."

Petra passed him the scissors. Shawn waited until the moon slid out again from behind the clouds. When it did, he bent low over the homemade candle and carefully snipped the extra yarn off the top.

"OK…light another match."

A flame flared in the darkness.

Shawn held out the canister of ski wax. Petra held out the match. The flame touched the green yarn. It flickered. And flared. Then settled down into a small, greasy, sputtering flame.

"It's burning!" exclaimed Shawn. "It worked! It actually worked!"

"Let there be light!" said Petra.

A gust of winter wind snuffed out the candle.

"Or not," said Shawn.

Stuck Between a River and a Hard Place

"Light it in the tent," said Petra, "out of the wind."

There wasn't enough room for them to get all the way inside the shelter. Shawn and Petra crawled forward until just their heads and shoulders were inside the flap of the doorway, then stopped, resting on their elbows. Hobart lifted his head and looked at them curiously.

"Okay," said Shawn. His teeth were beginning to chatter. "Light 'er up."

"This is the third match," said Petra. "There's only four left after this one."

She struck the match on the box. Shawn held out the candle. His hand shook.

"Hold it still!" said Petra. "I can't light it when it's moving like that."

"C-c-can't help it," said Shawn. "I'm c-c-cold!"

Petra reached out and cupped her hand over Shawn's, holding both the candle and his hand steady. She touched the match to the candle.

"There," she said. The glow from the candle reflected off the silver foil of the space blanket, lighting up the inside of the tent with surprising brilliance.

"Wow, cool!" said Tony. He pushed Hobart off and sat up. "Where did that come from?"

"Shawn made it," said Petra.

"Way to go, bro," said Craig. His voice was weak and raspy but he was smiling.

The light wavered. Shawn's hand was shaking uncontrollably.

"Whoa. Don't *you* go all hypothermic on me now," said Petra.

"S-s-s-sorry," said Shawn.

"I let you stay outside too long," Petra scolded herself. "I should have made you go in the shelter. You don't even have a jacket on!" Petra took the candle from Shawn's shaking fingers. She passed it to Craig. "Here," she said. "Hold this. And don't let it go out!"

"Okay," said Craig. He held the candle very carefully.

"Tony," said Petra. "You've warmed up a bit. I need you to come out here with me so we can put Shawn in the shelter. We have to get him warm right now."

Tony nodded and climbed carefully over Hobart.

"Hey, no hard feelings about me calling you a bear, eh?" said Tony, reaching down to give Hobart a tentative pat on the head. "You actually make a pretty good sleeping bag, you know that?"

Hobart thumped his tail.

Tony and Petra half-pulled, half-pushed Shawn into the tent.

"Here, Hobart," said Petra, patting a spot beside Shawn. Hobart grunted and heaved his heavy body over next to the shivering boy. Shawn burrowed down into the thick black fur.

They huddled in silence: Tony and Petra in the doorway of the shelter, and the two brothers inside, with the big black dog between them.

"I think it's actually getting warmer in here," ventured Craig after awhile.

Petra nodded. "A candle can make a lot of heat, and the space blanket traps it."

Shawn nodded. "I'm feeling better now."

"Good," said Petra, "Stay warm. Come on, Tony."

The two of them stood up, letting the flap of the tent fall closed.

Petra stamped her feet and slapped at her arms. Her fingers felt clumsy and stiff. She was cold. Too cold. She wondered how much longer it would be before they all needed a spot in the tent.

Petra strained to see through the darkness. The moon sulked behind a cloud. Silver light leaked out around the edges, but it wasn't really enough to see by. No other lights pricked the night. No searchers' flashlights, wobbling over the marsh. No firetruck lights, flickering red. Petra couldn't even see the tiny headlights crawling along the highway anymore. Instead, the riverbanks loomed higher than ever, fencing the Zodiac in behind a wall of darkness.

No. Not riverbanks, Petra suddenly realized. Cliffs.

The muddy, ice-capped banks had given way to ragged, rocky walls.

"Where are we?" Tony asked. He was staring at the cliffs too.

Petra shook her head. "Maybe somewhere between Lower Coverdale and Hillsborough...there's a high, rocky section around Scott's Hill," she said slowly. "Or..."

"Or?" prompted Tony.

"Or we could have passed Hillsborough altogether and be all the way down in Hopewell Cape."

"That's almost at the Rocks!" said Tony. The Hopewell Rocks were high cliffs that had been carved out into caves and weird shapes by the highest tides in the world. It was a provincial park now. Tourists came from everywhere to walk the beaches at low tide and marvel at the towering monolithic shapes.

Tony thought of something else. "The river isn't even really a river anymore by the time it gets to the Rocks...it's more like...the ocean. You can't even see the other side of it from the beach."

"Can you see the other side of the river from here?" wondered Petra. The two of them turned around and squinted through the murky gloom on the other side of the Zodiac. The moon peered sullenly from behind the cloud, but refused to show its whole face.

Tony blew out his cheeks in frustration and shook his head. "It's no good. It's too dark. I can't see the other side of the river, let alone make out any landmarks."

"This isn't good," said Petra.

"Well, maybe if we reach the Rocks, we could get out on the beach and find our way to the park area."

"It's closed this time of year," said Petra. "And even if we could find the beach, I don't think it would be a good idea to get out of the raft. We could slip on the rocks. Or we could get trapped by the tide. That would be bad."

"Very bad," agreed Tony. He remembered the big clocks at the Rocks that warned tourists when the tide was coming. Park officials herded visitors off the beach well before it was due to come in, and then closed off the only set of stairs leading down to the shore. During high tide, the water flooded the beach right up to the tops of the cliffs.

"Do you think the tide will be coming in soon?" he asked Petra.

"Probably," said Petra.

"And the tidal bore will come up the river?"

"Uh-huh."

"Petra?"

"Yes?"

"What do you think will happen when the tidal bore hits the raft?"

Petra didn't answer.

A Noise in the Night

"Petra?" asked Tony, again.

"Sssh!" Petra hushed him. "Do you hear something?"

"I hear water," said Tony. "'Water, water everywhere…'"

"That's not what I mean," said Petra. "I mean that sort of thumping noise."

"Aw, that's just my heart pounding," said Tony. "It always does that when I'm about to meet my doom, in the middle of the night, while adrift on a broken raft in the middle of a raging river. Don't worry about it."

"I wouldn't exactly describe the Petitcodiac as a raging river," said Petra.

"Oh, excuse me," said Tony. "How about a really grumpy river, then?"

"Knock it off," said Petra, "If you'd be quiet for two seconds you'd hear what I'm talking about."

They listened.

"Okay," said Tony. "Two seconds are up and I still don't—"

"*Sssh!!*" hissed Petra.

Shawn poked his head out of the tent. "Hey, do you guys hear something?"

"I'm telling ya," said Tony, "It's nothing. Just ol' Tony's terrified ticker…Hey, wait a minute—do you guys hear that?"

"*Sssh!!*" said Petra and Shawn together.

At first it felt like a low vibration coming from somewhere deep inside them.

It was a bit like a heartbeat. But faster. And louder. And it was getting louder still:

WUMP-WUMP-WUMP-WUMP-WUMP-WUMP-WUMP…

The air around them pulsed with the sound.

"I know that sound!" said Tony, "It's…it's…"

"A helicopter!" shouted Shawn.

"It's SAR! Search and Rescue!" shouted Petra.

Hobart came scrambling out of the tent. He turned in excited circles and barked at the night sky. Craig crawled out of the tent too.

"Are we being rescued?" he hollered above the noise.

"Yes!" shouted Petra. "Yes, yes, yes!"

A brilliant white light was slicing through the sky like a UFO, getting bigger and bigger and louder and louder. Like a great white eye, it was sweeping up the river toward them, punching a perfectly round hole in the night. The river flashed silver wherever the searchlight touched it. Then the helicopter was directly above them. For an instant, the brown water just to the right of them was lit up in a blinding stab of light.

And then it was gone.

"No!" wailed Petra. "No, no, no!"

But the searchlight was already shrinking into the distance. The helicopter disappeared into the darkness, heading back upriver toward the distant glow of the city. The *WHUMP-WHUMP-WHUMP* sound faded until there was only the *slop-slop-slop* of waves against the rubber sides of the raft.

"I don't believe it," said Shawn. He dropped his head into his hands.

"What just happened?" said Tony in a dazed voice. "Where did it go?"

"It didn't see us." Petra sounded shocked.

"It'll come back," said Craig, "it'll come back. Right, Shawn?"

Shawn's face was still buried in his hands.

"I don't know," he said, dully.

"Yes," said Petra, suddenly. "Yes—it will come back! Craig's right! A Search and Rescue helicopter always makes more than one pass over a search area!"

"Are you sure?" Shawn lifted his head and stared hard at Petra. Hope and doubt were both written on his face.

"Yes!" said Petra, excited now. "My uncle and I toured CFB Greenwood last year with the SAR volunteers. We learned all about helicopter rescue operations. It's really, really hard to spot people on the water, so they always sweep a search area twice. They'll be back—I'm sure of it!"

"Then we have one more chance," said Shawn, grimly. He stood up. His fists were clenched in determination. "We just have to make sure they see us next time."

"But how?" asked Petra.

"We could wave the candle," said Craig. He jabbed the little canister at the sky. Its tiny flame was just a pin-prick of light in the vast darkness. Shawn opened his mouth to say something, but before he could speak, a gust of wind had snuffed the tiny spark right out.

"Or maybe not," said Craig, looking at the candle sadly.

"It would have to be something way bigger and brighter to be seen from up in a helicopter," said Petra.

"Yeah, like a bonfire," said Tony.

"Exactly!" said Shawn excitedly. "We need to build a signal fire. How many matches do we have left, Petra?"

"Four. But we have nothing to burn. And no place to burn it, anyway. Unless we set the boat on fire."

"Um, I vote for not burning the boat," said Tony.

"There has to be a way," said Shawn.

"Whatever we do, we better do it fast," said Petra. "The helicopter could be back any minute."

Craig was still holding what remained of their homemade candle: a thin wisp of smoke curling from a blackened scrap of yarn in a small puddle of melted goo in the bottom of the can.

"Too bad we didn't have a bigger candle," he said.

Shawn looked at Craig. "That's it!" he said.

"What's it?"

"A bigger candle. We need a bigger candle!"

"But we don't have enough wax to make a big candle," said Petra.

But Shawn was shaking his head.

"Listen," said Shawn. "We can't light a big fire in the boat, obviously. It would either melt the raft or set it on fire…"

"Or blow it up," added Tony helpfully.

The others looked at him.

"That's a gas-powered motor," said Tony, jerking a thumb in the direction of the outboard. "You know— gas tank plus fire equals big *ka-boom*?"

"Right…uh, thanks for pointing that out, Tony," said Shawn. "Anyway, my point is that we can't light a fire in the boat. But we can light a fire *above* the boat…"

Craig's eyes widened as he caught his brother's meaning. "Like on top of a torch!" he said.

"Exactly," said Shawn.

"Great," said Petra. "So how exactly are we supposed to make a torch?"

Five minutes later, the space-blanket tent was in pieces. Craig sat with the blanket wrapped around his shoulders while Shawn and Petra examined the paddle that had been the tent's centre pole.

"How to we get it to burn?" asked Petra, running her hand over the smooth, varnished wood of the paddle. "I don't think it will catch if we just hold a match to it."

"No," agreed Shawn. "It won't. Torches need fuel at the top to keep them burning. Like rags soaked in oil or gasoline."

"Coming right up," said Petra. She fumbled through her first aid kit and pulled out the cloth bandages. She handed them to Tony. "Here," she said. "You can do the honours."

"Huh?" said Tony.

"You know," said Petra, "Rags plus gasoline equals our ticket home." She jerked her thumb in the direction of the outboard motor. "Gas cap's on the top."

Tony took the bandages. The moon peeked cautiously from behind the clouds. By its timid light, Tony unscrewed the cap on the outboard motor. He hesitated, holding the strips of cloth over the open gas tank. For an instant, even the wind seemed to hold its breath.

"Um, do I get hazard pay for this?" he asked.

"It's fine, Tony," said Petra. "Just don't light a match."

"Yeah," said Craig. "Or else—you know—*ka-boom...*"

Tony gulped.

He dipped one of the cloth bandages in the gas tank. "Don't try this at home, kids," he joked nervously. The gas soaked its way up the cloth. Tony passed it hastily to Shawn. "Here, you take it!"

Shawn wrapped the cloth around and around the top of the paddle. Then he held it in place while Petra pinned it with a safety pin.

"Guys," said Craig suddenly, "I think the helicopter's coming back!"

Race Against the Tide

Sure enough, in the distance a low *WHUMP-WHUMP-WHUMP* could be heard. The helicopter was returning.

"Quick!" said Shawn. "Light the torch!"

Hastily, Petra struck a match against the side of the matchbox. In her hurry, she pressed too hard. The match snapped in half. "Oh, no!" she said.

"It's okay," said Shawn. "Try again."

With trembling hands, Petra shook another match out of the box. She struck it. The flame flickered… and went out in a gust of winter wind.

WHUMP-WHUMP-WHUMP…

The helicopter was getting closer.

"Cup your hand around it," said Tony.

"I did," said Petra through gritted teeth.

"Just do it again," said Shawn. "Hurry!"

Petra shook another match into her hand. That left one match still in the box. She struck it. Nothing.

She struck it again, harder this time. Still nothing.

"Come on, come on…" Tony was chanting under his breath.

WHUMP-WHUMP-WHUMP-WHUMP…

Out of the distant darkness, a white light suddenly appeared in the sky.

"It's coming!" said Craig.

Petra struck the match again. Nothing.

"It's a dud!" she said in frustration.

"Try another one!" said Shawn.

Petra shook the last match out of the box. She looked at Shawn.

"It's now or never," he said.

Petra held her breath and struck the last match.

It flared…and caught.

"Cup your hand around it!" said Tony, "Don't let it go out!"

"I am! I am!" said Petra.

Carefully, she moved the match toward the torch.

"Uh, you guys might want to stand back," said Shawn to Tony and Craig. "Petra, watch out for your hair. If this thing lights up, it's going to burn like a rocket!"

Petra touched the match to the gas-soaked cloth on the paddle.

FWOOOOOOSH!

The top of the paddle turned into a fireball.

"Whoa!!" exclaimed all four kids.

"It worked! It worked! It worked!" sang Tony, doing a little jig in the bottom of the boat.

Shawn held the torch high above his head. It flared and danced in the night sky like a meteor.

"I feel like the Statue of Liberty!" he crowed.

"They'll see us for sure!" Petra clapped her hands.

"We're going home!" yelled Craig. "Wha-hooooo!"

"*Woof! Woof! Woof!*" barked Hobart, bouncing up and down on his front paws in excitement.

WHUMP-WHUMP-WHUMP-WHUMP-WHUMP...

The helicopter swept down the river toward them.

Suddenly Petra froze in mid-clap. She was staring downriver, in the direction of the distant ocean.

"Oh no," she said.

Three heads whipped around to look where she was pointing.

Rising above the blackness of the river, a white line had suddenly appeared.

It was a wave.

Its foaming crest stretched across the entire width of the river. It was bearing down on them like a freight train.

The tidal bore.

"Oh, man," breathed Tony, "it's going to broadside us."

It was true. Without a paddle or a motor, the raft was drifting sideways down the river. The tidal bore was going to hit them side-on.

"Will it flip us?" asked Craig, staring in horror at the approaching wave.

"Don't know," said Shawn. "Everybody, hold on!"

"What about you?" said Petra.

Shawn was still standing in the middle of the raft, holding the torch high above his head with both hands. He shook his head. "I can't let go of the torch—the helicopter's almost here!"

WHUMP-WHUMP-WHUMP-WHUMP-WHUMP!

The sound of the helicopter was deafening. But now there was a new sound. The roaring sound of rushing water.

"Here it comes!" yelled Tony.

"Hang on!" cried Petra.

Petra, Tony, and Craig crouched down, gripping the sides of the Zodiac. Tony reached out one hand and grabbed Hobart's collar.

Hands still holding the torch high over his head, Shawn closed his eyes.

SPLASH! The Zodiac bucked like a rodeo bronco.

Shawn felt his feet leaving the raft. The torch flew from his hands. The light vanished with a hiss as the flames hit the waves. Shawn heard Petra scream.

The sound of her scream was abruptly cut off as the Petitcodiac River closed over Shawn's head.

For a horrible, paralysing second, there was complete silence. The blackness was absolute. The cold encased him like concrete.

Then Shawn was aware of a dull roar in his ears. He flailed his arms and legs frantically. His head broke the surface. He opened his mouth either to scream or breathe, he wasn't sure which, but he couldn't do either. The cold shock of the water held his lungs in a vice.

The waves closed over his head again.

Shawn was sinking. A sleepy numbness was spreading through his body. He felt like he was falling through space. He looked up.

Above him, in the darkness, a light was glowing. Getting bigger. And brighter. Shawn wanted to touch the light. He reached out his hand. He kicked his feet. He struggled toward the light. His head broke the surface of the water.

Immediately there was an eruption of sound and noise. *WHUMP-WHUMP-WHUMP-WHUMP-WHUMP!*

A brilliant light was blinding him. A hurricane-force wind was beating down, whipping up the water in a biting hail of spray. Voices were shouting. Somewhere, a girl was screaming. And a dog was barking.

The river began to pull him back down. The calm, quiet blackness beneath the waves beckoned to him. Shawn began to let himself drift downward.

Suddenly something big and black canonballed into the water beside him.

Something was swimming around him, brushing against his legs.

Then a wet, furry body was pushing itself underneath Shawn's arm, buoying him up above the waves. His head broke the surface once more.

"Hobart?" choked Shawn. He hooked his arm around the big dog's shoulders. Hobart began to swim strongly, towing Shawn toward a circle of white light.

Then there was a man in front of them.

A man in a wetsuit, swinging from a rope that seemed to be hanging in space.

The man grabbed Shawn. He slipped some kind of a harness under Shawn's arms. The rope and harness began to rise, pulling Shawn and the man up, up into the sky.

Shawn struggled to see through frozen eyelashes. Everything was noise and wind and blinding light. The world tilted crazily far, far below him. Shawn tried to grab onto the rope, but his fingers were stiff with cold and wouldn't bend. He dropped his arms and hung limply in the harness. It was an odd feeling, spinning up through the night sky like that. He felt heavy and weightless at the same time. His mind felt frozen and sluggish. He couldn't quite remember what he was doing here, dangling from the sky.

Shawn looked down. He saw a river rippling like a silver ribbon. He saw a black dog swimming in tight circles in the water far below.

His mind snapped back to life.

"Hobart!" Shawn yelled. He flailed his arms frantically, trying to get a better view of the river. Where was the raft? Where were the others?

"Wait!" Shawn screamed. "Go back! We have to get the others! We can't leave Hobart in the water! *Craig! Tony! Petra!*"

The rope jerked and spun. The man was saying something...*Just calm down, son*...Strong arms wrapped around his, pinning him, holding him still. Up, up they rose, toward the waiting belly of the helicopter.

Cold, shock, and exhaustion flooded Shawn's mind with blackness and he knew no more.

An Unexpected Visitor

"Shawn? Shawn—wake up!" A voice was poking at him, prodding him toward wakefulness. Shawn opened one eye. He was in a white room.

And he was warm. Wonderfully and blessedly warm. He moaned and burrowed down further under the blankets.

Blankets? Where was he?

Shawn opened both eyes. His parents were leaning over him, worry evident on their faces.

"See—I told you he was awake!" Craig was bouncing on the bed by Shawn's shoulder. "Hey, Shawn! Was that helicopter ride cool or what?"

"What helicopter ride?" asked Shawn.

"Oh yeah," sniggered Craig, "I forgot—you fainted. Man, you missed the best part, Shawn. Helicopters are awesome! I'm going to be a helicopter pilot when I grow up for sure!"

"I did not faint!" retorted Shawn. He struggled to sit up. "Where am I?"

"You're in the hospital, sweetheart," said his mother, smiling weakly. "You're being treated for hypothermia, but the doctors say you're going to be just fine."

Shawn shook his head. Everything was so confusing. He tried to remember what had happened. *There was water and ice. And a boat…and a girl and…*

It all came flooding back. Shawn looked around in alarm. "Where's Petra? And Tony? Are they all right?"

"I'm fine," said a voice. Shawn looked up. Petra was walking into the room holding a bunch of balloons. She was with a tall man wearing a cast on one arm.

"You're looking much better," said Petra to Shawn as she tied the balloons to a chair next to the bed. She motioned to the man standing next to her. "This is my uncle, Daryl."

"You kids had quite an ordeal," said Daryl, "but your quick thinking and bravery really saved you."

"It was a team effort," said Shawn with a tired smile. "Speaking of which," he added, "where's Tony?"

"He's coming," said Petra, "In fact, he should be here any…"

"Excuse me, coming through, make way!" said a voice from out in the hall.

There was a crash, and the sound of something being knocked over.

"Oops, sorry about that!" came Tony's voice. There was another crash.

"Oops—sorry about that, too."

"You can't bring that creature in here!" said a nurse's indignant voice. "This is a hospital!"

"And this is a VID!" answered Tony's voice. "Excuse us, please."

And he marched into the room, Hobart leading the way.

The big dog leaped up on the bed and flopped across Shawn's lap. Shawn wrapped his arms around Hobart's neck and buried his face in the soft black fur. It was a moment before he could say anything. Then he lifted his head and grinned at Tony.

"VID?" he asked.

Tony grinned back. "Very Important Dog," he said. "What did you expect?"

"*Woof!*" said Hobart.

The three young people quickly piled onto the bed beside Shawn, all talking at once:

"It was amazing!"

"Terrifying!"

"The wave hit you and we all flew up into the air—"

"—tried to grab you—"

"Tony almost fell too—"

"Couldn't see you anywhere! The helicopter—"

"—hovering and a guy came down the rope wearing this SCUBA suit and plucked you right—"

"—we thought you were DEAD!"

"—got to sit in the cockpit and talk on the radio!"

"—and Hobart was still in the water—"

"—so the guy goes down and puts a harness on him and rescues him too!"

"And Hobart shook water all over the inside of the helicopter! Man, it was *so* cool!"

There was a breathless pause.

"Oh," said Shawn. "Is *that* all?"

A Chocolate River Celebration

Two weeks later, a thick white quilt of snow dropped over the town of Riverview. The winter sun had set, but warm light glowed from every window of the Mahoney household. From inside came the sound of voices, music, and laughter. Outside, a tall figure accompanied by a shorter figure and a bear-sized dog crunched up the snowy walkway to the house. The shorter figure reached up and rang the doorbell.

Almost instantly the front door was flung open by a grinning, blue-eyed boy.

"Hi Petra! Hi, Daryl!" Then he turned and called over his shoulder: "Hey, guys—they're here!"

"Hi, Craig," said Petra, stepping inside and pulling off her toque. "Are we late?"

"Not at all," said Craig's mother, hurrying over to take their coats. "You're just in time. Come right in."

"Thank you for inviting us, Jean," said Daryl as Craig's mother took his coat. "This was a fine idea. A most excellent idea, in fact."

"It was the least we could do," said Mrs. Mahoney gratefully. "I have to warn you, though—the menu was the boys' idea." She smiled and led Daryl and Petra (closely followed by Hobart) into the living room.

The room was full of people: firefighters, police officers, paramedics, volunteers, and the Search and Rescue helicopter crew...everyone who had helped in the search for the children had gathered together in the cozy house.

Above the mantle, a homemade banner was taped to the wall. It read:

THANK YOU, CHOCOLATE RIVER RESCUE HEROES!

A cheerful fire crackled and snapped in the fireplace.

At the coffee table, Reg, the driver of Rescue 10, was playing a game of chess with a young police officer...the man who had tried to reach the boys when the ice floe first broke away from the bank. In another corner, a tall firefighter named Butch was perched on a stool, playing a foot-stomping tune on a fiddle. He was being accompanied by Tony, who was blowing enthusiastically into a kazoo. Shawn was busy examining a high-tech, hand-held GPS locator belonging to one of the Search and Rescue crew, while across the room, Craig was arm wrestling the helicopter pilot.

A chorus of hellos greeted Petra and Daryl as they entered and there was much back slapping and hand shaking before everyone settled down again.

In the kitchen, Mr. Mahoney was bent over a large pot simmering on the stove. He was wearing an apron that read *Don't forget to kiss the cook!* in pink letters. The smell of chocolate wafted through the house.

"Come on!" said Craig, steering Petra and Daryl toward the dining room. "We're just getting to the good stuff!"

In the middle of the room was a long table spread with a rich brown tablecloth, and on the tablecloth was the most delicious parade of chocolate desserts imaginable: chocolate cupcakes, chocolate-chip cookies, chocolate brownies, chocolate fudge, chocolate cheesecake, and chocolate cream pie.

"Get it?" asked Craig, waving toward the table. "It's a river of chocolate!"

Just then Tony's mother walked over, adding yet another dessert plate to the table. Craig picked up a long, thin, chocolate-covered bar from the plate and offered it to Daryl.

"Try one of these," he said. "They're made with ice cream."

"Mmmmm," said Daryl, making the treat disappear in one bite. "What do you call those things?"

"Frozen fingers," said Craig, grinning.

Daryl laughed. "And how are *your* frozen fingers doing?" he asked. Craig held up his hands and wiggled his fingers. "Still have all ten of them," he said. "No harm done. Shawn and Tony have all theirs, too. The doctors said we were lucky that the frostbite wasn't too serious. We're all better now."

"Glad to hear it!" said Daryl.

"Make way for my masterpiece!" said Mr. Mahoney grandly, carrying a large tray of golden pastries to the table. Reg followed close behind him carrying a bowl of steaming-hot chocolate sauce.

"Wow!" said Tony, bounding over. "What are those?"

Everybody crowded around the table.

"These happen to be my world-famous chocolate ice cream puffs," said Mr. Mahoney proudly. "The recipe was handed down to me by my grandfather," he added.

"What's in them?" asked Shawn, licking his lips.

"It's pastry with a scoop of frozen ice cream inside," said Mr. Mahoney. He turned and Reg ceremoniously passed him the bowl of homemade chocolate sauce. "And then," he continued, "they're flooded with chocolate."

He tipped the bowl and poured a thick ribbon of chocolate sauce over the ice cream puffs.

"Oh, yeah!" said Tony.

"I call it Chocolate River Surprise," Mr. Mahoney said modestly.

"Now *that's* the kind of river I'd like to go swimming in!" said Craig.

"Wait!" said Shawn, as everyone was about to dig into the delectable desserts. "We almost forgot the drinks!" He disappeared into the kitchen and reappeared with a tray of frosted glasses. In each one, a scoop of white ice cream bobbed in a frothy brown liquid. "Chocolate floats! Get it? Chocolate *floats*?"

"Oh brother," said Tony, slapping his hand to his forehead.

Much later, bellies stuffed with chocolatey sweets, everyone bundled up into coats, boots, hats, and mitts. Together they walked down the dark, snowy street. At the bottom of the hill, they crossed the main road and walked up the footpath, onto the bridge. There, they all stopped to look out over the railing at the now-peaceful river. Under the night sky, cradled between its banks, the water was streaked with starlight. The people on the bridge stood in silence for a moment, listening to the waves whisper secrets to the snow. Then they turned and walked away.

Walking back up the hill, the children lagged behind the grownups. They trudged in silence for a bit, side by side. Walking between Tony and Craig, Shawn suddenly reached out his arms and hooked both boys in an affectionate headlock.

"Ack!" squawked Craig.

"Hey, whachadoin'?" protested Tony.

"I was just thinking," said Shawn as the two shorter boys struggled beneath his armpits, "that it's really kind of cool…"

"What's cool?" spluttered Tony.

"That my heroes are also my best friends."

Looking over top of Craig's head, Shawn smiled at Petra. She grinned back.

"I know exactly what you mean," she said.

At that moment, Craig and Tony wormed free of Shawn's hold. With whoops and yells, they tackled him, knocking him into the snowbank.

Then Petra was firing snowballs and Hobart was barking and the night erupted into laughter and happy shouts.

And in the distance, beneath the darkness, the river slept.